THE ROOTS HAVE DUG
INTO MY HEART

PETER FUGAZZOTTO

ALSO BY PETER FUGAZZOTTO

The King Beneath the Waves

The Witch of the Sands

Black River

Five Bloody Heads

Into Darkness

Alien Infestation

The Rise of the Fallen

The Cellar

Skin

1

JESSIE DID NOT NEED another shot of bourbon to feel better, but she was already on that slippery slope. The one where she imagined that every drink would bring her exponentially more happiness. For her, that slope was furrowed with a well-worn, familiar path.

It was a Saturday night and the Western was crowded. At the bar, locals in their cowboy hats mumbled and complained over their Coors. On the other side of the room, tourists flocked at tables, laughing too loudly over their Jack and cokes. The tourists were the worst, making a show of casually dropping the peanut shells on the floor, dressed in their outdoorsy fleece jackets and shoving their heads together for selfies. Music crooned out of the jukebox and a couple of tourists whirled drunkenly, stomping just out of beat.

Jessie looked up at the clock on the wall behind the bar. She had promised her mother she would not be out late but it was already was past midnight and since Maya, Jessie's daughter, must have been tucked in and asleep at that point, it did not matter when she got home. She ran her fingertips over the two empty shot glasses in front of her. She could not see the harm in one more bourbon. She wanted to have fun. She deserved it. It was Saturday night, after all.

So, when the out of towner she had been eyeing through the mirror behind the bar lay down his pool cue, swaggered away from his friends, and slid onto the empty bar stool next to her, she could not suppress her smile.

She glanced at his thick fingers drumming the bar. No ring. She could only imagine what he would be like. The last tourist she had picked up at the Western had been disappointing. It was as if he did not know how to do anything but lay on top of her, sweaty and grunting. This guy with his easy smile and relaxed eyes promised to be different.

"Lining up the shots? Where's the party?" he said, gesturing at the empty glasses on the bar. He winked. "I'm Mac."

"Are you just going to talk, or you going to buy a girl a drink?"

"You certainly know what you want."

Mac bought bourbon shots and fancy beers in bottles. He was from the city by way of San Diego, here on the coast for a wedding, he said. Old college friends. Jessie wasn't surprised that he worked in tech in the city. His shiny leather shoes, silk shirt, and fancy phone gave him away. He rattled on about VC and AI and other things that did nothing to impress her.

Every weekend his kind found themselves out on the coast for a Northern California farm style wedding. They were lured in by the fog-laden hills, the photographic waters of the bay, the rolling hills spotted with cows. It was everything the city was not. They dreamed of an idyllic country life, the kind promised in lifestyle pieces in magazines or online. Jessie's mom talked about fixing up their barn and making their property a wedding destination, maybe it would give Jessie something to focus on. But she couldn't imagine suffering brides and their mothers, and anyway, she had a three-year old she was raising by herself. She had no time for anything.

"This place is so beautiful. We went on an amazing hike today. Right out to the sea," Mac said. "You must love living out here."

"I lived in Portland for two years. Now that place was fun. Fun, fun, fun."

"If it was so fun, why'd you move back?" Mac walked his fingers across the bar towards her wrist.

"Husband became an ex-husband."

He turned his empty shot glass up into his lips, his pink tongue darting out for the last drops. "You're too young to have been married. A girl like you."

"You got any coke?" she blurted.

He failed to hide his laughter. He popped off his barstool and huddled with his friends. They all looked back at Jessie, laughing, whispering among themselves. She could see them evaluating her, and she knew she would pass their judgment. She always did, blonde hair, bright eyes, enough of a figure. She looked good at night, in a smoky bar. It hid the wrinkles, the weariness around her eyes, and the discontent.

One of his friends pulled his fist out of his pocket and laid it on Mac's palm. He returned, leaning into the bar.

"We rented a Suburban. Comfy backseats, tinted windows. We can have our own private party."

Five minutes later, they hurried out the side door of the Western and cut through the crisp air to the gravel lot across the street where the car was parked. The fog had slipped back in, muting everything. Even so, a block away, she could see where the town ended at low fence posts and barbed wire, behind which a neglected pasture rolled down towards the marsh and the black ink blot bay.

He held open the door to the Suburban. "Ladies first."

Inside, he quickly went to work, cutting the coke, drawing it into four neat lines on a magazine. She snorted first, then he did, then each hit their second line.

"You and me, now, baby. You and me." His eyes were wide.

Jessie sucked, then flared her lips. "Mac, Mac, do they call you Big Mac?" She reached across the seat and slid her hand up his chest. He bit his lip. She could see his anticipation. She grabbed his shirt and jerked him towards her.

They kissed, hands running over each other's bodies. He tasted like steak. He was not shy, touching her breasts and cupping her hips. Jessie's heart raced, and her breath quickened. She slipped her fingers down between his legs, smiling as his cock stiffened.

They pulled apart, panting like animals, fingers at their own clothes, zippers and buttons, opening their burning skin to the cold night.

"I got a kid," she whispered.

"That doesn't matter."

"My ball and chain."

Mac laughed. "I got my own."

"A boy or a girl?"

"A wife."

She slapped him so hard that the back of his head thudded against the glass of the car.

"Fuck you!" she said. "You cheating son of a bitch."

He curled his lip at her and for a moment she braced for his hand, memories of her ex flashing before her. But Mac stayed his hand. His lips trembled, his voice lowering to a controlled hiss. "You're one crazy bitch. What's wrong with you?"

"You have a wife. You'd cheat on her? I hate your type."

"Jesus Christ, get the hell out of here." He reached across her, careful not to touch her, and pushed the car door open. His lips kept moving, cursing without sound.

Jessie stumbled out of the car, buttoning her shirt and pulling her jacket back on. "Son of a bitch." She kicked the side of the car.

She pulled a cigarette from her pocket, lit it with trembling fingers, and walked. Within a few moments, she had left the center of town and reached the residential district. Houses filled the right side of the street, and on the left, past a leaning barbed wire fence, the grazed wetlands, glowing white from the moon in the darkness, gave way to the black stain of the bay, and beyond that the silhouette of wooded hills rose.

She was halfway down the street when she heard the voice. It twined with the wind hissing through the tall marsh grasses. The voice was low, plaintive, and at first, she thought it was a coyote's muffled yips but then she heard words, but words she could not quite make out.

Jessie froze in her tracks, straining to listen, her rising breath competing with the crying. She felt suddenly alone. Her skin goose bumped and, for a moment, she thought about running straight back to the bar. She turned back to the sound of the voice. A tangle of blackberries rose on a small hillock in the marsh. Where had that come from? Had she not seen it before? The hillock drew her eyes. It drew everything towards it with an almost visible magnetism as if it sucked the land into it, as if the whole world, and Jessie, were being pulled towards its strange gravity.

Her knees buckled and she almost pitched forward. How much did she drink tonight?

Behind her, the houses were suddenly far away, the street a hundred yards wide. Their yards overgrown with dead grass, windows black and empty, paint and wood sloughing off as if the houses were made of melting wax.

"Jessie." A word formed from the wetlands.

She should not have been seeing these things, or hearing voices. She was clean of the heroin, the acid, all that heavy shit. She had been clean since she had been back from Portland. She should not have been tripping like this. Unless Mac had slipped something in her drink or cut something stronger in the coke.

She glanced over her shoulder to make sure that he had not followed her.

She whimpered. She wanted to scream to unleash the growing terror she was feeling but she was afraid that she would not be able to stop. The tangle of blackberries burned dark in her sight.

Someone was out there in the swampy waters. Someone who knew who she was.

She stumbled to the fence and when her hand found a wooden post, hundreds of flies suddenly lifted, filling the sky in front of her, buzzing around her face, sticking to her lips. She swatted and they cleared away for a moment but then they raced back, cloaking her, pushing into her nose, pinging against her eyes.

She closed her eyes for a second, and when she opened them she was on the other side of the fence, her feet sinking in the muck of the wetlands, the grasses twined and pulling around her ankles, clouds of flies rising from stagnant pools. The town behind her seemed miles away, the few visible lights shrinking away like stars.

"No!" Her scream broke whatever insanity she was imagining, and she found herself back on the other side of the fence, the beckoning voice lost to the wind, the land solid beneath her feet, the houses normal again.

She wasted no time and hurried away, back to the Western, back to the same bar stool, Mac and his crew gone, and she ordered another shot to steady her nerves and to drown out this nightmare of an evening.

2
_____

THE NEXT MORNING Jessie did not get out of bed when she was supposed to. She lay beneath her comforter, drifting in and out of wakefulness, first woken by the distant alarm from her mother's room, then by the stomping and voices of Maya and her imaginary companions. Her head throbbed. She wanted a glass of water to clear the film from her tongue. But the bed was warm, the kitchen too far, so she closed her eyes.

She woke again to her mother looming at her bedroom door. She peered in, white hair haloed by the hall light. Her mother had aged during the years Jessie had lived in Portland, deteriorating as if time suddenly accelerated. "Maya's watching TV now. She's been fed. I'm leaving for the market." Her mother crossed her arms and tapped her foot on the floor. "Do you hear me?"

"The market. Maya."

Her mother stood there long enough to make Jessie uncomfortable. She sat up in the bed. Pale morning light crept into the room through the gap between curtain and sill. Cold air slithered beneath the comforter. Sitting up was not good. The edges of the room tilted. She couldn't remember how many drinks she had the night before. The cocaine had not helped either. While the extra shots of bourbon had burned out the hallucination she had been having at the edge of the marsh, they had given her a massive headache. Even now, hours later, she was still half-drunk. She cursed herself silently, hating herself for not stopping at two drinks, for going to the car with Mac, for even going to the bar at all. "I'll get up soon."

"Jessie, sweetie."

"I know. I'll call the Station House, see if Martin can bring me back on for a couple of shifts." She could not imagine waiting tables again. She'd be too exhausted to have the energy to spend time with Maya or go out and blow off steam.

"You came in really late last night. Too late. We agreed that you could come back here on the condition you get your life back in order. Live by my rules. You can't be spinning out of control like you did in Portland. We know how that turned out. You've got responsibilities now. You've got a three-year-old daughter. You can't be living like that again. The judge warned you."

"You're going to be late."

"Call Martin."

Jessie waited until the sound of her mother's truck faded up the driveway before collapsing back onto the mattress. Even lying down did not help. The room still tilted. Her stomach gurgled loudly. She rolled over several times before closing her eyes. The bite of whiskey lingered on her breath, sharp and sickening. She swore she'd be clean for the rest of the week, not go out. The hangover was never worth it.

Her mother had left the door open and Jessie heard the nonsensical voices from the cartoon, screaming and laughter. The bitter smell of coffee drifted from the kitchen. It would still be hot in another hour. Her mother wouldn't know when she got out of bed. Maya would be fine with the cartoons. They were far more entertaining than Jessie could be in her state. The kid could sit entranced in front of the television for hours.

She pulled the pillow over her head. Fragments of the night

before returned to her: Taylor Swift from the jukebox in the Western, the shots at the bar, that moment she slapped Mac.

Her memories drifted back further, to that morning six months ago when Paul finally admitted he was sleeping with the waitress. How days later, Jessie had stood on the iron bridge wondering how quickly the Willamette River would swallow her, whether the cold would eat her pain. She thought about how lucky she was when she had been arrested for the DUI that the police had not found the heroin tucked in the baggie under Maya's car seat. After all that she went through, she needed to return home, to recharge, to get her feet back under her, a fresh new start.

Now she was back in Nova Albion, living at the family farm, though it was not much of a farm anymore. After the crash in milk prices, the herd had been sold off and thistle and broom consumed the pastures. When Jessie's father died, her mother was forced to find a job in town. When Jessie left years before, it had been to escape the despair of a dying agricultural community, and now returning it was as if she visited the land of the dead. Each additional day she stayed, the harder it was to escape its pull. She wondered if that was what her hallucination was really about the night before, the horrible gravity of this dying place.

Those thoughts disintegrated into blackness and sleep, and when Jessie woke again, it was to sharp, bright wedges of light in her room.

The laughter and music from the cartoons were louder than when she had passed out into sleep. She pulled the pillow over her head, but it did not help. Then she heard Maya crying, a steady stream beneath the sounds from the television.

Jessie threw the pillow to the floor and sat up. The floorboards were icy beneath her bare feet.

"Maya, baby, come here. Come into bed with Mama."

Jessie waited, and then stood. The room tilted and then

righted itself. She needed that coffee now. A little more sleep would have helped, too.

"I'm coming, Maya. Mama's coming."

She pulled her blanket off the bed and wrapped it around her shoulders and then shuffled into the living room. Frantic cartoon characters screamed and laughed on the screen. Cereal fanned across the couch and the floor, the empty box crushed flat as if it had been stepped on.

Jessie grabbed the remote from the coffee table and muted the television.

"Maya, baby, where are you?"

Jessie looked again at the spilled cereal, the indentation on the couch where Maya had curled up. The sound of her crying ended with the muting of the television making Jessie think her ears had been playing tricks on her and that Maya had not been crying at all. But still she heard an echo of the crying, a sound that existed just beneath the wind outside, beneath the ticking of the clock, beneath her own breath and Jessie suddenly remembered the voice that she heard in the field the night before. A disembodied cry in the darkness.

Jessie's heart suddenly began pounding and her breath raced as a wave of panic washed over her.

"Maya!"

She dropped the comforter from her shoulders and ran into Maya's room. Books on her bed, stuffed animals on the floor, the blinds in her window bent as if she had been looking out into the fields.

Jessie ran to the bathroom, her mother's room, the kitchen. She climbed the steep stairs to the attic. The door groaned as it opened. The light revealed boxes, keepsakes from her own childhood, her father's book collection.

She checked all the rooms again, tearing open cabinets, looking under beds, ripping clothing out of closets.

"Maya! Maya!" Her jaw trembled and she clutched her hair in both fists. She ran back into the living room.

That was when she noticed the front door was not closed. It was slightly ajar, the light from outside a bright ribbon.

She yanked the door open. The cold wind pummeled her. Her eyes watered. Fog twisted through the pines covering the mountain on the other side of the bay. The grasses sloping towards the water had turned brown and red with the coming of winter, everything sharp and muted at the same time, the ground drawing life back in before the darkening days. She sucked in several deep breaths, took two steps forward, and collapsed to her knees on the porch.

The barn loomed on the other side of the drive. Maya could be there. She could have gone to visit the goats or look for the dog. She always wanted to pet the dog. She could be there, hidden in the shadows.

Jessie pushed herself back to standing and stumbled towards the barn, the gravel sharp against her bare feet, and she kept telling herself that Maya was in the barn, that Maya just wanted to find the dog.

But she knew it was a lie. She knew her daughter had disappeared.

3

"WE NEED TO STOP TALKING, stop standing around, and find Maya." Jessie perched on the front porch, fists clenched so hard her arms trembled.

Sheriff Reyes held a pen and notebook. In the driveway, the lights of his cruiser flashed blue and red. "Jessie, I need you to relax. I need you to take a few breaths. Calm down. Talk me through this again."

Jessie wanted to scream. It had been half an hour since she had stumbled back from the barn and called 911, and fifteen minutes since the sheriff and deputies had been combing through the house and searching the edges of the property.

"She's not here. She's gone. We need to stop all this talking and look for her. We need to find her."

"Jess, take a deep breath." Reyes was in his mid-fifties, and his uneven eyes gave him the appearance of always looking next to her, rather than at her. He had cornered Jessie the first week she had returned from Portland and told her he didn't want any big city problems being brought back to Nova Albion. "When was the last time you saw Maya?"

"Last night. At dinner."

"Last night?"

"Don't look at me like that. My mother put her to bed and made her breakfast this morning. She was watching cartoons this morning."

"Did you see her this morning?"

"What kind of question is that? What are you asking? Why are we wasting time like this?"

"Your mother saw her this morning?"

The deputy came up to the foot of the porch steps. "Barn's clear."

Reyes turned back to Jessie. "That handyman, Troy, you seen him around the property much? You ever take your daughter down to the encampment on the Flanders property?"

"Why would I ever bring her down there?" She had gone down to that section of the Flanders ranch where he allowed itinerant day laborers to live, an encampment of trailers and vans and blue tent shelters. Mostly she had gone there because her mother had asked her to find Troy, to knock on his trailer door, to get him to fix sagging fences or to round up the goats that had broken through the fence and wandered into the marsh. She had also gone there to buy weed. But she had never brought Maya with her.

"I have to ask. It's my job. You know I'm trying to help you. I'm trying to figure out where she might be." Reyes turned on his shoulder radio. "Maggie, I'm need you to get Flanders on the phone, get permission from him so that we can have someone come onto his property and talk to the folks at the encampment. And I'm going to need a search and rescue team out here at the Milanos. Right away."

"Did Troy do something? Did he do something to Maya?" asked Jessie.

"Breathe, Jessie. Do you have any idea where your daughter might have gone? Has she talked about anybody in particular lately? Any strangers? Anyone giving her too much attention? Or has there been anywhere she has been talking about going lately? Her father is still in Portland, right?"

Jessie couldn't handle it any more. She burst into tears. This was not helping. None of this was helping. Her daughter was missing, and they were wasting time asking questions. They needed to be looking for her.

She stared at the barn, the pasture where the goats lined up against the fence, the untended land beyond that sloped down towards the marsh. Morning fog still lingered, weaving through the grasses. The water of the bay lay as still as a black mirror.

Memories of the night before dug into Jessie's consciousness like tendrils pushing through rotting earth. She remembered how she had heard the voice beneath the wind, the hillock of washed out grasses, the gravity of the tangle of blackberries as if it were a black hole.

"She's out there somewhere, I know it."

A car engine whined, gravel popped beneath tires, and her mother's truck skidded to stop in front of the porch.

Her mother jumped out of the truck and ran up to the porch. "Maya's gone? Have you looked everywhere? Sheriff, have you looked everywhere in the house?"

Reyes explained the situation to her, told her they could not find her and that a search party was forming, and that it was best if the two of them waited on the porch. He'd have more questions and he wanted them to be here in case Maya came back. Then he went to his car and he and the deputy talked in hushed voices.

Jessie's mother wrung her hands. "Did you not get up like I asked you?"

"I can't talk about this right now."

Her mother's voice dropped low and her lips trembled. "I told you that when you came back here you needed to live under my rules. Stay away from the drugs and the alcohol. I rescued you once. That was your chance. I never should have let you come back. I should have taken Maya and let you die on the streets with a needle in your arm."

"Thanks, Mom. I love you too. Do you really think I wanted this to happen?"

"You just didn't want to change. You want to chase your selfish desires no matter where they lead, no matter what the consequences. Well, now look where you've found yourself. You're still drunk and god knows what else, and you couldn't drag yourself out of bed to be with your daughter. I can't leave you alone for ten minutes. I thought you'd realize how important your daughter was and see that you were given a second chance. I thought once you came back here, you would change, and realize that you had someone else to live for."

"Fuck you, Mom. You don't know anything about me. I love Maya more than anything else in this world. She's the only good thing I have. I was just tired. Is that a crime? I closed my eyes for a moment. Who left the front door open? You tell me that. She should have been there on the couch. But the door was open, Mom. You left the door open."

"I can't even talk to you, Jessica. Look at what you've become. I don't even see my daughter anymore. How did I ever love you?"

Her mother hurried into the house and slammed the porch door behind her. Reyes and the deputy looked up from a map spread on the hood of the car and then toward the sound of another police car rolling down the driveway.

Jessie shut her eyes and dug her thumbs into the back of her neck. Sharp needles drove into her shoulders and she felt like her head was going to explode. She wanted to close her eyes and she wished, when she opened them again, the police would be gone, Maya back, curled up on the couch, and this nightmare over.

But she could not turn back time and everything that had been so precariously stacked was now falling over, piece by piece, and crashing to the ground. Her world was falling apart.

The wheels of a firetruck squealed at the top of the drive as it turned off the highway. All of this was unreal, as if out of a movie.

Jessie's breath shortened and her stomach tightened. She suddenly felt as if she were about to throw up. She sucked in air. She needed to do something. She could not just stand here and wait.

As she stepped off the porch, the wind suddenly buffeted her, hitting her so hard that she almost tripped. It hissed through the dry grasses, waves racing across the pastures.

Her hair whipped across her cheeks and Reyes and the others turned their eyes from swirling dust. The deputy caught the map as it lifted from hood.

Jessie was halfway to them when she heard the sound of the voice beneath the breath of the wind, the sound of her daughter crying, a plaintive wail coming from the fog-laden marsh.

And before she knew it, Jessie was running, past the shouting officers, through the opening in the fence, and into grasses, following the wail of her daughter.

4

JESSIE RAN into marsh chasing the sound of her daughter's voice. Behind her, Sheriff Reyes yelled for her to stop. She knew what she was doing was not right.

But she would not let the one good thing in her life slip away. Not without a fight. Not without trying. She would not let Maya slip away like everything else had. Not like the promise of love, nor the hope of a vibrant life in Portland, nor the touch of nirvana from the needle plunged in her arm.

Maya was different. She was bright, even when Jessie was darkest. She offered real hope. All of those other promise and dreams had been lies. Pain. Addiction. Delusion. Maya was real. Something that would pull Jessie out of her world of despair.

But it was even more than that. It was the primal connection, that compulsion that was built into the genetic code of all living things, what it meant to exist. A mother had to protect her child. Jessie had no choice. She had to find her.

It had not been her fault that her daughter had wandered out of the house. Jessie had only been napping a bit. It was no different than any other morning. Maya should have been watching cartoons. Jessie's mother was the one who had left the door open when she left for work.

Regardless of whose fault it was, her daughter was still missing and, worse, the police, rather than fanning out to begin the search, were content with asking endless questions and waiting for more first responders to arrive while wringing their hands. Every moment they waited, Maya slipped that much further away.

As Jessie plunged into the marsh, fog rose from the grassy mounds and muddy rills of the tidal wetland. The mist grew thicker, forming into a solid wall and making her feel as if she was about to cross into another world. She hesitated, suddenly fearful. Tentatively, she extended her hand and, as fingertips, hand and wrist vanished into the white, wetness draped across her skin. She drew her hand back to her chest, and shivered. The skin on her hand and arm was red and goose bumped.

Then the voice rose again, lilting beneath the wind, and Jessie's throat tightened, and pushing aside her fear she plunged through the wall of fog.

As she was enveloped by the mist, the shouts of the officers faded, the twittering of the marsh birds died, and the hum of traffic from the highway muted. Even her own gasping retreated as if it travelled a great distance instead of hissing from between her lips.

The borders pressed in, the sky a low ceiling, the edge of the world ending at arm's length. She turned back towards the house and the barn. The flashing red and blue lights pulsed faintly, almost imperceptible, and the silhouettes of the buildings merged into a single shapeless dark gray swath.

She heard the cry again, born from the fog, and ran towards it.

She did not get more than a few steps in before she tripped. Her foot clipped a clump of grass that suddenly rose out of the murk and she fell hard, stones biting into her knees and palms.

She sat back, clenching her jaw so that she would not cry out. Her hands burned, and she looked at them. The skin bled, cut by the sharp grasses she had grasped at as she had fallen.

She wondered whether she should turn back. It was not too late. The rescuers had to be there now. They would manage this better than she could. The way things were unfurling, she would be the one lost in the marsh for days. Then, the thought of Maya accidentally plunging into the bay tightened her chest. She was young, could barely swim, the water too cold. She would not last more than a handful of breaths. The water would swallow her.

Jessie leapt up and plunged further into the swamp.

After a few more minutes, she realized she was lost, utterly disoriented. She had no idea where she was going, not even the general direction she was moving, and worse, she was no longer sure whether she had even heard Maya's voice or whether she had imagined it. She could be walking in circles or even heading straight back to the barn. She held her breath. The wind moaned. Maybe some other sound carried on it, a plaintive call beneath the surface but the more she strained to hear it, the more she was sure it was the wind itself, a guttural hiss, a rattle of dead stalks, unseen animals in the grasses.

She ran several steps, stumbling, blind in the fog, legs burning, gasping until it felt like her chest was going to burst.

She stopped, bent over, hands on knees, and spit up saliva. She wiped her lips with the back of her hand and staggered forward. She sucked in air, panting like an animal. She could smell the whiskey coming back up on her own breath.

She swore she would give up the booze and partying. No more coke. No more heroin. None of it.

"Maya!"

She wandered through a maze of winding trails, rising and falling over grassy mounds and small hillocks, always returning to black water and the disturbed reflection of herself, unable to tell whether she descended towards the bay. The ground was soggy and she slogged through mud and puddles. The place stunk of stagnant water, the sour rot of the grasses. She glanced over her shoulder. The barn, the flashing lights from the police cruiser, even the sun were consumed. Lifeless gray.

Eventually the fog thinned enough that she could see a dozen feet around her and she began to discern trails in the land, corridors of grasses flattened as if something unimaginably heavy had slithered through the yellow and brown grasses. Slime, mucus flecked in black, coated the grasses. She could not help but envision some tentacled creature dragging itself along the earth.

"Maya," she called and her voice echoed back, tinny, flat.

Jessie cursed.

Then she heard a faint sound. She stopped and turned trying to orient herself to it. She held her breath. There. She heard something. It was her own name.

"Jessie, come back. We found her."

Her breath shuddered in waves out of her chest and she ran towards that beacon of a voice. The fog thinned and the sound grew. Ahead, the mist bled once again red and blue with the lights of the police cruiser. Finally, she could distinguish the silhouettes of the barn and the house and people, shadows materializing.

But before she broke the fog, she heard a different sound. She stopped and glanced behind. Not her name this time, but a cry that made her skin prickle. The mists swirled, almost becoming substantial. A touch of wind on her cheek, wrapping around her wrist, beckoning. Jessie felt the physical gravity of the marshland, as if the world was drawn into a whirlpool, draining towards a single point, pulling her towards it.

She took a step towards the lights and shadows of her home. But she was held back. She looked down at her feet. The tall yellow grasses had wrapped around her ankles and calves.

"We found her," one of the first responders called.

She kicked her feet free and ran, the buildings and the figures solidifying before her, gathering color until she broke from the grasp of the fog and burst in the bright bold light of the morning. The sun was so strong that tears filled her eyes, but maybe those tears were also because Maya was sitting in the back of an ambulance, legs dangling, the knees of her green panda pajamas mud soaked, twigs and grasses tangled in her hair.

Jessie ran to her, past Sheriff Reyes and her mother, and scooped her daughter into her arms, squeezing her to her chest. She tried to say something but the words would not form, the bubbling joy eating them.

Maya was so cold and the dampness from her pajamas transferred to Jessie's arms.

"Where did you go? You're never supposed to wander off from the house. You almost scared your mommy to death. You know you're not supposed to do that. I'm never going to let you go."

Maya smelled like mud and standing water.

Jessie tried to be there in that moment, alone with her daughter, but her mother was berating her from over her shoulder and Sheriff Reyes was saying that he needed to talk to them and the paramedic was asking Maya to sit back down so he could get her temperature.

Jessie did not want to let her daughter go. Not now and not ever. She swore to herself that everything would change, that she would be the mother that she was supposed to be, that she would cold-turkey cut out the booze and drugs, and she would live her life for her daughter.

She embraced Maya a moment longer, as tightly as she could, before turning back to the paramedic.

She lowered Maya to the ground, and spun her so they were facing each other. She looked at her daughter through tear-blurred eyes, and said, "Your mama loves you more than anything in the world, and I'd do anything to protect you. You know that, don't you?"

Maya nodded woodenly, lips pressed together. As the paramedic picked her up, Jessie saw a pale tendril, like a white root, tangled in her daughter's hair and as she tried to pluck it out, Maya pulled her head away. Jessie would get it out later, when she had Maya alone all by herself, when everything was back to normal. When she could finally start living the life she was meant to.

5

OVER THE NEXT THREE DAYS, Jessie did not leave her daughter's side. Maya disappearing in the marsh had woken a fear that Jessie could not shake. Everything that had been her world, even as miserable as it was, was almost ripped away. She knew Maya was the only good thing in her life, the beacon of light in the darkness that had descended on her. She needed to hold on to that. Because she could not return to that darkness.

Five years ago, Jessie had been seeking light, any light, to escape her dead end life in Nova Albion. Paul, a wild musician with a voice like honey, whom she met after he played a set at the Western, had filled her with hope. She remembered that day when she left for Portland looking into the car side mirror at the reflection of her mother and father standing in the yard, shrinking as the distance between them grew. Nova Albion had nothing for her. A dead farming community at the edge of the continent where the bitterly cold sea ate the land. No work, no love, no hope. So she had latched onto Paul's guitar string dreams and raced north to Portland with him, where he said gigs waited and all their dreams were ready to come true.

That wonderful world of light did not last long.

She should have seen it coming. The signs were there. She saw it even in that first month in Portland, when everything seemed all right.

She drifted back to the memory of one of those moments after a night of drinking, of getting higher than she had ever been in her life, of her wanting another taste.

She sat in the donut shop, their regular morning dive, him on the other side of the table, paper napkin crumpled in his fist. She had gnawed the end of the red plastic stir straw flat, as if that could somehow relieve the tension that was building up.

Paul dipped the last wedge of his donut into his cup of steaming coffee. He plunged it until it had become a half-disintegrated lump between forefinger and thumb.

"You won't be able to drink the coffee afterwards," she said. "You're gonna have mush floating in it."

He pinched one side of his face. "It all gets mixed together down in my stomach in the end." The stubble on his face which looked good the night before was now a little too long, and he was looking haggard rather than rugged.

She glanced at her reflection in the hazy window next to their table. Maybe she was a little puffy around her eyes, and she would benefit from brushing the tangles out of her hair. But she was really not worse for the wear. Unlike Paul. He looked worn out, older than his years. Maybe his nights of wild living had piled up more precariously. She wondered if she would always be immune.

Through the window, people lined up along the opposite sidewalk, smoking cigarettes, leaning on their shopping carts, hands in pockets, bouncing their feet against the cold. They waited for the homeless shelter to open, and the bags of food they'd all receive. They lined up here every day, never free from the gnawing pain in their bellies. Those people were worse for the wear, she thought.

An old lady with rags wrapped around her feet, toes blackened, held a bottle in a paper bag and tilted it so that the amber liquid sloshed. Then she handed it to a tottering old man with a short white beard. Jessie looked at those feet again. Dirt or rot. Hopefully the former. Either way it was hard to look at, especially while they were eating.

She jabbed donut crumbs from the wax paper onto her finger and popped them into her mouth.

"What kind of lawyers are your parents?" she asked.

"Why you got legal problems you haven't told me about?"

"Just want to know more about you, that's all. Fill in the gaps."

He blinked at her, as if just noticing her sitting across the table. "We're only having fun, you and I. It's better that way." He reached across the table and covered her hand with his. "And it's not you, you know. Nothing wrong with you. Me, though, I'm a bum. I've got some pretty bad tendencies. Relationships don't ever work out for long with me. Don't be sad. I just don't want you to get your expectations up about me. Yeah, both my parents are lawyers, but me, not such a good catch."

His hand felt icy over hers, so cold that it sent a shiver up her spine, and she wanted to pull her hand away from his. But she did not. She kept it beneath his despite the discomfort. "Who said I wanted to catch you? I was making small talk, that's all. Need something to do to fill the space between fucking."

He laughed, shaking his head. "The country girl in the big city. You don't need to put on airs with me. I like you just how you are. A little rough around the edges, my uncut diamond. And don't worry about me running off right away. I like you." He squeezed her hand. "I'm having a good time. You're having a good time, too, right? So what more is there to say than that?"

He took a long low, steady sip of coffee. "Mmm, mush coffee." He dragged a napkin across his lip and then dropped it in the coffee. "Let's get out of here. I want to get high again. What do you say?"

"I've been waiting for you to finish that coffee." She imagined the flame of the lighter, the stem of the pipe warm between her lips, that first rush, and the smoke snaking towards the ceiling. She needed a taste because she was not satisfied and she needed more.

Back then, fucking him, getting high, being free from home. Those were her beacons.

Now, the one shard remaining was Maya, and Jessie had nearly lost her.

So she vowed she would lay off the drinking, stop being tempted by drugs, and be the mother that she was supposed to be.

For those first three days after Maya came back from the marsh, Jessie did the best that she could. Late at night, she carried a sleeping Maya from where she curled on the couch, to Jessie's bed where she would wake several times to touch her daughter's hip or listen to the sound of her breathing. Clean from bourbon and drugs, Jessie woke clear headed to the sunrises and birdsong. She filled her daughter's bowl with cereal and milk, and one morning even made Mickey Mouse pancakes. Every day, she took her to the small playground behind the store in town, huddling on the benches with the other mothers while the kids careened about screaming. In the evenings, Jessie resisted the craving to head out to the Western and instead sat Maya on her lap and ran her finger over the pages of picture books and watched the cartoon animals leaping and laughing across a kaleidoscope of colors flashing from the screen. She went as far as making polite conversation with her mom.

But even with life getting back to normal, something was wrong. Jessie did not want to admit it, but something had been wrong ever since Maya had disappeared and come back from the marsh.

On the fourth morning after Maya had disappeared Jessie could not ignore it any more.

That morning, Jessie's mother had been reluctant to leave, lingering at the front door, letting cold seep into the house. The air, wet with fog, slithered in the house, licking at Jessie's bare ankles. She wanted her mother to go.

"I'm awake. I'm here. Go to work. You have nothing to worry about. Maya won't leave my sight."

Her mother clutching her purse returned to the kitchen table where Maya, still in her pajamas, bent over her bowl, slowly swirling the cereal into the milk.

"Stop playing with your food and eat," Jessie said. Maya was usually so hungry in the morning and Jessie wondered where her appetite had gone. She had hardly been eating for days. And, on top of that, Maya had barely said more than a few words this morning, and each day seemed to be drawing further within.

Her mother hugged Maya. "Going to miss you, my little angel." She straightened quickly, nose scrunched, looking at Jessie. "And give her a bath, she still smells like a swamp."

"She had a bath last night."

"Then give her another one. Can't you smell it in her hair?" Then her mother left, slamming the door so hard that the windows in the house shuddered. Jessie did not let out her breath until her mother was gone, her truck rumbling up the drive. Then Jessie relaxed.

"What are we going to do with you, baby girl?" Jessie squatted next to Maya and stared at the soggy cereal. "You don't like the cereal anymore? You gotta eat something. Are you not talking to your mama anymore?"

Jessie returned to the counter and sipped from her coffee. It was no longer piping hot, barely warmer than her lips, and the milk clumped at the top of the mug. Jessie pulled the sugar jar from the counter. Empty. She cursed. She'd call her mom later to pick up sugar from the store. Or maybe she would head into town with Maya, but that was so much effort, and her mother was right. Maya did smell like the marsh, like standing water, and she would need a bath, and with Maya, that would be a production. By the time they were ready to get out of the house, it would be lunchtime and half the day would be gone, just to get sugar. It seemed like too much work.

She turned back to Maya and sniffed. Her daughter smelled like sewage. Even if she had gotten into something in the marsh, that had been several days ago and she had several baths since then and the clothes she had worn had already been washed. She should not have smelled like that.

Jesse pulled out the chair next to Maya and slumped into it.

"What's in your hair?"

A smooth white tendril, two inches long, poked from the back of Maya's head. Jessie caught it between both fingers and tugged, but it would not come free. She pulled again, grabbing it firmly. This time when she pulled, Maya's skin lifted with it. Jessie leaned in closer. She could see tiny roots dug into her scalp. Still the tendril would not come free.

"What did you get into? Were you rolling around in the dirt?"

Jessie tightened her grip, braced her other hand, and pulled slow and steady. The tendril lengthened as if it furled beneath her skin. She pulled it until it grew to half a foot in length, with still no end of it in sight, and then Maya suddenly turned her head and the tendril, pale and white, snapped.

"Don't do that," said Maya. "Leave me be. Mama."

Jessie ran her fingers over the spot from where she had pulled the tendril. The skin beneath the hair was puckered and a drop of dark liquid, black and oily, formed there. She dabbed it with a napkin and sniffed it. It smelled like swamp water.

"You need a bath again, and we are going to wash your hair twice. Three times. As many times as it takes to get you clean." Jessie fought to keep her voice under control. She felt frustration bubbling beneath the surface and it threatened to rise as sharp words and insults. Maya deserved to be treated better than that.

"And no more running out of the house. I don't know what I'm going to do with you."

Jessie got up and tossed the tendril into the garbage beneath the sink. While she was there, she paused. She looked out the window across the yard and beyond the fence to the marsh. The fog was thick, the grasses fading quickly into oblivion.

She remembered the fear and dread she felt as she had wandered into those mists, the cold, wet earth pulling at her, the grasses twined around her legs. She shuddered.

Maybe she and Maya needed to get out of Nova Albion. It no longer felt like home. But she really had nowhere to go. Portland was out of the question. The fact that she didn't have any money limited their options.

She sat back down next to Maya who continued to aimlessly stir her cereal. Jessie took the spoon from her hand, scooped up soggy flakes, and brought it to Maya's mouth.

"Aren't you hungry, sweetie? You need to eat something today."

Maya shook her head, lips pressed tight.

"Then the bath it is."

6

THE BATH DID NOT HELP. Despite ample hot water, half a bar of soap scrubbed in with a washcloth and a pile of shampoo bubbles, the smell of the swamp lingered on Maya. After the bath, Jessie spritzed her with a bit of perfume to mask the odor but the combination of sweetness and rot only made the smell more unbearable.

Back at the kitchen table, Maya again stared at a bowl of fresh cereal, this time not even picking up the spoon. Jessie stood over her shoulder watching the milk slowly disintegrate the flakes until the inside of the bowl was a pasty mess. She choked back her rising frustration.

"Let's go out. Get pancakes or eggs. We've been cooped up in this house for too long."

Half an hour later, they arrived at the roadside diner in Tocaloma, the next town along the coastal highway north of Nova Albion. It would have been quicker to head into Nova Albion to get something to eat but the market where Jessie's mother worked was across the street from the diner, and Jessie did not want her mother seeing them and coming over on her break, hovering over them, sniffing at Maya, harping about how she needed a bath, and couldn't Jessie even do that one thing right.

Since it was midweek and during the hours between breakfast and lunch, the diner was not busy. Jessie picked a table by the window and after the waitress laid down their menus, Jessie spread out an assortment of broken crayons and a coloring sheet.

When the waitress returned, Jessie ordered. "We're hungry today. Let's see. How about an order of scrambled eggs with bacon, and I want the griddle potatoes. And French toast, straw-berries on top. And, Maya, you're hungry, right, baby girl? You're going to eat something? A short stack of the blueberry dollar pancakes and bring lots of syrup."

"And drinks?" The waitress squinted at her pad.

"A big glass of orange juice for her. And for me, oh what the hell, I'll have a beer."

"You want beer?"

"It's close enough to lunch, right?"

The waitress glanced at the clock on the wall and shrugged.

When the waitress went to the kitchen counter to place the order, Jessie turned to Maya. Her cheeks were sunken and her skin pale, the blood drawn away from her cheeks. Hints of dark circles were forming beneath her eyes. And still that odor.

Jessie could only imagine how her daughter looked to the other people in the diner. They must have thought she was sick. Jessie felt a rising headache. She rubbed at her temples, the back of her neck. A dull pain seated in her head, diffuse enough that she could not quite place it. The rubbing did not help.

When the beer arrived, Jessie drank deeply, sucking down half the glass. She wished they served something stronger here. Bourbon or vodka. She needed the burn of that first shot of hard alcohol to smooth her nerves. Everything was getting jumpy again. She knew what she really needed to dull the pain and damp down the rising anxiety but she wanted to be clean for her daughter, and had stayed away from that stuff since coming back from Portland.

Maya dragged crayons across the paper, filling the page with large, heavy blocks of color, thick with wax, and seemed unconcerned with staying within the lines or coloring the barnyard figures.

"Try not to draw so much on the table."

Maya looked up, glaring, crayon clutched in her fist.

"Food will be coming soon. You must be hungry. I get a little angry, too, when I'm hungry. There's a word for that, you know. Hangry. Have you ever heard of that word? It's funny, isn't it?"

Maya had already turned her attention back to the paper, madly smashing the wax crayon across the paper.

Jessie tried to talk with Maya, about the weather, about what they were planning to do for Thanksgiving, about how she wanted to start looking for a job soon, but it was if Maya heard none of it. All she could focus on was the bleed of color, the heavy rough lines.

Jessie bit her bottom lip. She finished the beer. Still, she felt the dull ache in her head, now at the base of her skull. She felt like her spine needed to be cracked.

Finally, the food arrived.

"I hope you girls brought your appetites."

The waitress balanced plates of steaming eggs with potatoes and bacon, pancakes stacked high and dusted with powdered sugar, and browned French toast with slices of strawberries layered on top.

When she tried to slide the pancakes in front of Maya, the girl would not stop scrawling on the page. Jessie asked her to take a break. Maya kept driving the crayon into the paper.

"Here let me clear some space." Jessie moved aside the water and put the condiments on the next table so the waitress could set the food down. "I'm sorry about that. She's being intolerable."

"Kids are kids. What can you do?"

But Jessie saw the faltering smile, the too-long glances at the chaos of color and lines on the paper, at the empty beer.

"Anything else you need you let me know, okay, hon?"

"If you had whiskey, I'd be lining up shots."

The waitress forced a closed lip smile and walked away.

Jessie dug into the eggs and bacon, watching over each forkful, waiting for Maya to push aside the crayons. The drawing was a tangle of dark, angry lines.

"Are you not hungry, Maya? We came out all the way here to get you something special to eat. I know how much you like pancakes."

"Maya does not need to eat anything," she whispered as she bent over the drawing.

Jessie clenched her jaw and silently counted to five. This was getting ridiculous. Her daughter was embarrassing her and acting spoiled.

"How about the French toast then? We can put syrup on it. Maya likes syrup."

"I'm going back to the mud."

Jessie gasped. "What?"

Maya pressed a crayon so hard against the paper, it snapped in her hand.

"Enough!" Jessie clamped her hand over Maya's and tore the crayon from her grip. "You're acting like a spoiled little brat. I'm not going to let you watch cartoons today until you take a bite of something."

Jessie scooped a forkful of eggs, stood up, and bent over next to Maya. She ignored the stares of the waitress and the other patrons. She held the fork in front of Maya's pressed lips.

"Go on, now. Eat! Take a bite."

Maya dug her fingers into the paper, crumpling it. Her eyes narrowed.

"Stop being a bad girl. You need to eat. I bought this for you."

She shook her head.

"I am going to count to three."

On two, Maya lunged, mouth open, and bit Jessie's hand.

Pain flashed in her hand and raced up her arm, electricity lighting up her nerves. She dropped the fork and choked back a scream.

Maya's teeth broke skin and tore muscles. Jessie pulled back but Maya held tight, blood coloring her lips and chin. The pain had turned into a flood of fire where the teeth clamped down.

She needed to get her hand free.

She slapped Maya hard.

She opened her mouth and Jessie tumbled back onto the floor. The skin on her hand was torn open, the semicircle of teeth marked in gushing blood.

"You monster! I should have left you in the marsh. I never should have come for you. We'd all be better off."

The waitress was kneeling alongside Jessie, lifting her hand and wrapping it in a towel. The other patrons watched, eyes and mouths wide. Maya was bawling, face streaked with tears and bright red where Jessie had slapped her.

Jessie pressed a trembling hand over the towel. Blood soaked through, each beat of her heart sending shearing pain into her hand.

"I'm going to call 911," said the waitress. "This isn't right. Any of it."

"No, leave us be."

Jessie grabbed her purse from the arm of her chair and threw twenties at the table. Then she scooped Maya into her arms, and charged out of the diner, the late morning light blinding off the windshields of the cars parked in the lot. She stumbled to her car.

Within moments, they were racing south back towards Nova Albion, and their home. Jessie could barely see the road through her tears. She rolled down the window and gulped in air until her

37

heart no longer felt like it was going to burst out of her chest. Her hand pulsed with bolts of fire.

"Why, Maya, why?"

She glanced back through the mirror. She wanted an explanation. She wanted something. Anything. Maya sat quietly in her car seat licking the blood from her fingers and lips, smiling.

7

WHEN JESSIE GOT HOME from the diner, she locked Maya in her room and guzzled whiskey to numb the pain in her hand. That didn't work, so she dug out her stash of weed and smoked until she could barely keep her eyes open. Then, she drank more whiskey. Finally, exhausted from the horror of what had happened at the restaurant, she passed out on her bed. She woke in the mid-afternoon to once again find her mother standing in her bedroom doorway. Behind her mother, cartoon screams and laughter boomed from the living room.

"We can't go down this path again," said her mother.

"I'm tired. What I had to deal with this afternoon."

"You're drunk. You passed out. I can smell the weed."

Jessie raised her bandaged hand and explained what happened in the restaurant. "And this is my fault too?"

"It was an accident."

Jessie laughed and rolled her eyes.

"You make the bed that you lie in," her mother said.

"Oh my god, you are somehow pushing this on me. Why did I ever come back here?" She tore the sheets from her and sat up. She gagged on bile rising and lay her throbbing hand in her lap.

She should not have drunk so much, but her hand was killing her and she was upset with what had happened in the diner. Worse though was the memory of looking into the rear-view mirror and seeing her daughter hungrily licking the blood from her hands and face. It was pure horror, and she needed the whiskey to clean that image from her mind.

Her mother waited in the doorway, arms crossed high over her chest. "You came back from Portland because you had no choice. And that's the way you lived your life. What did you expect? You dropped out of college halfway through the semester. You ran off with that cheating bastard. A musician. A goddamned musician. I warned you about him. How did you think things would ever work out in Portland when you had no one around you? And then you brought Maya into the world, exposing her to your sordid lifestyle. The drugs, the alcohol. And you wonder why she runs away, why she lashes out, why she refuses to eat. You're a monster in her eyes. Not a mother."

"I'm here for her now."

"Are you really? Stinking of booze most every day. Barely able to get out of the house. And when you do, I get a call that you hit her, in public, made the poor thing bleed. You're lucky Sheriff Reyes wasn't called."

"She bit me."

"After you hit her. That's what they told me."

"That's a lie. She bit me first. There's something wrong with her."

"No. You hit your daughter. Your daughter! There's something wrong with you. You need to get help. And if you don't soon, if you don't turn things around, I'm going to make sure that you cannot hurt that child anymore."

"Get out of here!"

Jessie waited until her mother left to finish her shift at the market and the whine of the truck faded up the drive. She climbed back into bed and wrapped the covers around her, pulling the warmth to her. She closed her eyes.

She would be better to Maya. She would spend time with her. She would be with her. They would put aside whatever it was that lay between them. They would be close, unlike how she and her mother had become.

She just needed sleep. She needed the day to start over again.

She woke to afternoon light streaming in through her windows. She glanced at her phone. 4:45. She had slept for another two hours. Her mother would be home soon.

She threw aside the covers and got dressed. It was a struggle to zip and button her pants with only one hand.

When Jessie walked into the living room, she knew something was wrong. The television was black, the blanket on the couch a tangle, and the front door open again.

Jessie's breath caught in her throat, and she stumbled as she ran, her knees weak. Not again. Not again, she thought.

She burst through the front door.

The light was blinding. Everything turned to white. She could smell it. The marsh. The rot. The sourness. The death.

She ran blindly towards the fence and the grasses beyond.

She was halfway there when she heard Maya's scream and an angry deep voice. Not from the marsh. But from the barn.

Jessie ran into the barn. It was dark. Even so, she could see the two figures, Maya struggling, hands pinwheeling, her attacker holding her up by the hair.

Jessie closed the distance and as she was almost there, she saw that it as Troy, their handyman, the vagrant that the police had been looking for on the day that Maya had disappeared.

"Let her go!"

Troy glanced up for a moment and then pressed something in his free hand against Maya's neck and she screamed like a feral creature.

Jessie rained her fists on him, and surprisingly he let Maya go immediately. Jessie swept her daughter into her arms and smelled burnt flesh, the malodorous cloy of the swamp. She stepped away from Troy and into the light and saw a red mark on her daughter's neck where he had burned her.

With a cross.

The skin welted, and black ichor pooled around the wound. As Jessie reached out, the oil sucked back into Maya's skin.

Maya squirmed and broke free. Jessie reached out helplessly as her daughter ran into their house.

She turned to Troy as he emerged from the shadows of the barn.

Troy Morrow had seen better days. His dirty blonde beard was mostly just dirty. His eyes were marked by the wrinkles of a man much older, his lips chapped and cracked.

He swayed slightly at the opening of the barn, one hand steadying himself on the frame. She could smell the beer on him.

Despite whatever damage and decay to which he had subjected himself, he carried himself as if he had once been confident and vulpine. But that posturing vanished in fit of coughing, and when he finally drew in a breath, his eyes were watery, as if brimming with sorrow, and his body stayed hunched, legs bowed and fingers curled as if arthritic.

"What is wrong with you, you sicko? You burned my daughter's neck."

He tossed something in the air to Jessie and caught it. A small iron cross, as cold as ice, lay in her palm.

"The iron burned her. And that," he said looking past Jessie towards the house, "that thing, is not your daughter. Haven't you noticed?"

8

JESSIE DID NOT CALL the police after Troy drove off in his van. She did not phone her mother and tell her what she had caught Troy doing. She did not panic even though that would have made the most sense.

His words stuck with her. She had been noticing that something was wrong with Maya. Ever since she came back out of the marsh, the smell, the lack of appetite, the way that she had attacked Jessie in the restaurant, all these things added up to something seriously wrong and made Troy's word ring true.

She spent the rest of the day in the house, the cartoons blaring on the TV. Maya sat on the carpet in front of the screen, tearing her dolls apart at the limbs and putting legs and arms in her mouth, gnawing on the plastic, spitting shreds onto the carpet.

"Maya."

She sat on the floor, a doll's dress bunched in her fist, pressed to her teeth.

"Hey!"

She looked up.

"You're hungry, aren't you?"

She had become even more hollow-cheeked with dark blue rings forming under her eyes. She stared, unblinking, her eyes glazed as if a slight film had formed over them.

"Come into the kitchen. We'll find something for you."

Jessie left her there and opened the fridge. She pulled a packet of raw ground beef from the shelf, peeled back the cellophane, and plopped the bloody meat on a plate.

When she turned around to call Maya from the living room, she was already standing behind her. She held a limbless doll in one hand, teeth marks on its bare body. Jessie jumped back, unable to breathe for a second, and as she bumped into the counter, the meat slid from the plate onto the floor.

Maya dropped on four limbs and like an animal dug into the raw meat with her mouth, slurping, lips smacking, and when she was done, she licked the plate, pushing it along the floor until it butted up against the cabinets. When it was shiny clean, she stood, elongating her body, stretching her fists above her, arching her back, and shaking her head.

Jessie dug her fingers into her palms and choked back a scream.

"That's it. No more."

Maya sucked her lips into her mouth. She stared at Jessie for a little too long, her gaze dropping to her hand and the blood-stained bandages. Then she skipped back to the living room and lay down on the floor in front of the TV.

Jessie wrapped her arms around herself fighting the trembling that overtook her body. Troy's words returned to her. *That thing is not your daughter.* Jessie wanted to scream. What kind of crazy idea had Troy introduced into her head? This was Maya. This was her daughter. She had run off and gotten lost in the marsh. Yes, she had been acting strange, smelling foul, since she had returned. Maybe she was just sick with something, some infection beneath her skin that made her stink like rot, some disease that made her crave raw blood.

Jessie swung around to the sink and vomited. When she was done she stuck her mouth under the running faucet, and splashed water on her face.

She returned to the living room.

Maya was curled up on the floor in front of the TV, asleep.

Jessie knelt down beside her.

This was her daughter, her one and only, her sweet little joy. Something was wrong, that was all. She'd call the doctor and get an appointment the next day. He'd figure out what was wrong. He could do tests. Surely, he must have seen something like this before. What was happening to Maya had to have happened to other children before. This was her daughter.

Maya lay there, her body curled, eyes darting wildly behind paper-thin lids, whimpering like a dog barking in its sleep, stomach bellowing with her frantic breathing.

Jessie brushed Maya's hair away from her face, and as she did so, she noticed that the blister on her neck, the angry red welt from the cross that Troy had pressed against her skin, was gone. Her neck was smooth, all signs of trauma gone.

Jessie thought for a moment that maybe it could have been the other side of her neck but she knew it wasn't.

"What's happening?" she whispered.

That thing is not your daughter.

She remembered the burnt skin, the blistered flesh, and her own feeling of shock when she held the ice-cold cross in her palm. Cold does not burn.

She still had the cross. She slid her hand in her back pocket and pulled it out. It was so cold that it felt wet between her fingers. She pressed it against her bare forearm. No red mark. No blistering skin. Nothing.

Maya mumbled something in her sleep, words that sounded familiar but in a language that Jessie did not understand. They seemed to make the air tangle around her, as if it became visible, manifesting in strands that slithered into substance. Jessie shuddered.

The iron burned her.

Jessie hesitated, holding the cross above her daughter's neck, not because she was uncertain what would happen, but because she knew what would happen and she realized that once it did, there would be no turning back. The membrane that masked the world would be removed, and she would never be able to return to the illusion that she'd known.

Holding her breath, she lowered her shaking hand. As she brought the cross closer, Maya's skin reddened, in the shape of the cross, and black ichor worms wiggled beneath her skin. An angry red welt rose. Maya, still asleep, swatted Jessie's hand away.

Jessie fell backwards. The room tilted but she steadied herself. She could not draw in a full breath. Her vision speckled as if she were about to pass out. She grabbed the arm of the couch and pulled herself to her feet. She ran to the front door and jerked it open.

Fresh air washed over her and she gulped in breaths, the black spots shrouding her vision vanishing. She turned to look into the house. That thing, not Maya, lay on the floor, blood sated, that thing that wore her daughter's skin. Even in sleep, she squirmed, wiping her hand across where the cross had welted her flesh.

Jessie blinked. She still could not draw in a full breath. She stumbled down the gravel drive, away from the house, away from that thing.

Her heart drummed so hard she could hear it, and she thought her head would explode, but then she heard it in the wind, in the howl that keened across the dead grasses of the marsh. A voice so small that it could have been lost: the cry of her daughter.

9

LATE THAT NEXT MORNING, when her mother was home and angrily banging pots and pans in the kitchen, Jessie went to go find Troy Morrow. He knew what was going on. He had pressed the iron against Maya's neck for a reason. He could help Jessie figure all of this out, because right now it made no sense at all.

Jessie drove to the encampment where Troy and the other itinerant workers lived. It was on the northern part of Old Man Flanders' ranch, so Jessie needed to drive out to the main road, head north, and then turn onto the access road. The gate to the access road was open, the chain locked around the post.

Her car tires rumbled over the cattle grate. The fields looked like they had not been used as pasture in some time. Upright husks of thistle littered the property in broad swaths of gray. When Flanders was still alive, he kept herds on this land, and had battled the thistle, but with him gone and his heirs squabbling and trying to sell the ranch, the weed consumed the land. The remaining oat grass had turned brown with the end of the summer, waiting for the rain and renewal. It had grown knee high, heavy at the top with seed, falling flat in places as if an invisible beast had stormed meandering paths through the fields.

Jessie stared, thinking of the trails she had seen cutting through the marsh.

She inched her car over a small rise and reaching the summit, she braked to a stop, surveying the pasture that swept to the north and the south. Wide open land. Despite the absence of the cows, she still smelled manure. In front of her, where the gravel road ended, the encampment sat at the edge of the marsh on a wide, flat spot, cupped by a thick wall of willows and blackberries.

Cars had been parked in the shape of a semicircle to face a fire pit built with stone and chunks of concrete. One or two of the cars were so rusted and weed-choked, they looked as if they had grown out of the ground. Blue tarps stretched between several of the vehicles and the rest the camp was littered with piles of wood and pallets for burning. There were lawn chairs, clothes hanging on a line, a rusted grill, and black garbage bags overflowing with aluminum cans and beer bottles.

She drove her car to the edge of the encampment and then reversed it into a small gap in the bushes so if she needed to drive away quickly, she would not need to turn the car around. A woman and a man, thin and disheveled, stared at her through the grimy windshield of a pickup. Beer cans lined the dashboard.

Jessie climbed out of the car and strode towards the camp.

The air was alive with movement, with the heat of the sun-warmed grasses swaying against the cold air racing from the ocean. Summer had faded and the descent into winter had begun. The camp smelled of salt, sour blackberries, and wood smoke. High above, lost in the bright sky, a hawk screamed.

The man in the pickup watched her coming, and he kicked the door open and ran, beer in hand, into a low tunnel in the wall of blackberries. Another two men suddenly emerged from the shadows between cars and took off after him. Jessie could only imagine why they might be running. Her mouth was suddenly dry. She could not swallow. She wondered if she was making a mistake coming here alone, unannounced and uninvited. Strangers were not always welcome.

But she thought again of Maya and the cross. She needed to find Troy.

Jessie stopped at the fire pit. The wind gusted suddenly causing the ashes to rise into a white dervish. She shielded her eyes with the crook of her elbow.

The woman sitting in the truck drained a beer and climbed out. She was horse-faced, a few teeth missing, the others black edged. She held a palm up against the sky, her veins forming rivers of blue running down bone-thin arms.

"We ain't doing nothing wrong here. The farmer's son says it's all right for us to stay here. We ain't doing nothing stronger than a little drink and smoking some weed." The needle marks on her arms told another story.

More people emerged from their cars, from the shadows beneath the tarps, from rustling tents. Maybe two dozen in all. People living on the edge. Children, hip high, hiding behind their mother's legs. Men, countries away from their homes.

"I'm looking for Troy Morrow."

The woman pointed towards a white van. "Troy, Troy! You got a visitor. You hear me?" She whispered to Jessie. "He can be a little high strung if you come on him without warning if you know what I mean. Troy! Wake on up. A lady here to see you."

One of the other men finally spoke up, clearing phlegm from his throat every couple of words. "He's not here. He and Rodrigo got some work at the Triple Two Dairy. Probably going to the Western afterwards. You can find him there."

The woman chuckled then stopped suddenly, hands scratching, creating red lines on her bare arms. "You ain't going to throw us out, are you? Most of us trying to get honest work, and just need a place to stay. Times are tough. We don't make trouble. We keep to ourselves, best we can."

Jessie walked to the van and pounded on the door. She

49

pounded again. The van was edged in rust, a bicycle hooked onto the back, a blue tarp tied over a bundle on the roof.

Jessie peered through the tinted windows. He had leaned reflective material against them but she could look in the gaps.

Books stacked on the floor. Books about the occult, satanic rites, witches, alchemy, and local indigenous mythology. She glimpsed the title of one, a textbook about police investigative procedure.

Flyers for missing girls were taped to the far wall. Dozens of them. Flyers from different states. MISSING. HAVE YOU SEEN THIS GIRL? Young faces staring at Jessie. They circled a map with arrows drawn in thick red marker ink.

Gravel ground behind Jessie. She turned, afraid that the fleeing men had returned. The horse-faced woman stood behind her rubbing the needle marks that lined her arms, palm hissing over skin. Jessie remembered that insatiable hunger, and the glazed look in the woman's eyes brought back the memories of the comfort of being lost in the dream world that the heroin brought. Jessie fought to not imagine herself as this woman. The birth of Maya had steered her away from that path.

"Troy, he's one of the good ones," said the woman. "Sure he's got his issues. We all do." She chuckled and again scratched red lines into her arms. "But he helps people. He's got this gift and he helps people, people whose children go missing. Is that why you're here? Someone go missing?"

10

HALF AN HOUR LATER, Jessie arrived at the Western looking for Troy.

Even in the middle of the day, the bar was dark. Jessie paused at the doorway, eyes adjusting. She scanned the room, gaze stopping at the pool tables, making sure that guy from the other night, Mac, had not overstayed his welcome.

She pushed inside. Country music crackled. She winced at the sharp mix of stale beer and bleach. Where her shoes did not stick to the floor, they crunched peanut shells. Light filtered in through high windows clouded with grime and dirt. Deer and boar heads lined the paneled walls.

Jessie leaned on the bar, bought a shot of whiskey, and after finishing it, looked in the mirror. Troy sat alone at a table in the corner, a half-finished bottle of Coors in his hand, a book spread open before him.

Jessie ordered two Coors, ignored the tired glances of the ranchers looking up from their pint glasses, and sat in the chair opposite Troy.

He watched her slide a bottle across the table.

"I always hope that I'm wrong," he said. "I honestly do. Once in a while, I am."

"What did you do to Maya? With the cross?"

He looked past her, at the bar, to the door. For a moment it looked like he would get up and run.

He gnawed at his lower lip and blinked several times before dabbing the corner of his eye with a knuckle. "Your father was a good man. Gave me work on the farm, but he was also a man who had the gift. He could sense the waves beneath the surface. Do you know what I am saying? I think you do. He and I had many a long conversation about the hidden patterns, the threads in common among the various schools, and how the changing of the houses will provide a space, a gap through which unnamed things can emerge. That is what we sensed. The signs were there, the lining up of the stars, the patterns of the birds lifting over the bay, the shifting in the land. When these signs line up, they let us know that we should be paying attention, that something has broken through the veil."

"I'm not interested in any of this nonsense. What happened with Maya? What did you do to her?"

"Better to let things unravel like they are destined to."

She reached across the table and squeezed his wrist, the bones beneath her grip felt as fragile as a bird's. "You burned her with cold iron. Then it healed. I put the cross to her. Her skin turned red. What's happening?"

"You said you aren't interested in all this nonsense. If that's the case, I have nothing to say. And you're hurting me."

She released her grip. "Fine. Then tell me what you have to."

"There's more to all of this than we can see. We're presented with a flimsy veil that we call reality but there is more behind that veil. That's what I'm after. I'm a scholar and a bit of a detective. Nothing formal, of course. I investigate things of a, shall we say, occult nature. The territory beyond the map, so to speak. This is for you."

He reached into his jacket and handed her a bracelet made of acorns, sea shells, and bottle caps, twisted copper and twine. It smelled of seaweed.

"You don't have to wear it. You can if you want." He lifted his wrist to show his own. "It's a charm. To protect you. You don't have to actually wear it. You can put it in your pocket. Best to keep it with you at all times, but especially if you are wandering out into the fog and the forest."

"Protect me from what, Troy? What exactly am I supposed to be scared of?"

"If your father could see beyond the veil, I imagine it's in your blood too. I don't really need to tell you what you're seeing. You know what it is. There are people, you know, and, well, other things. Maybe you have not figured out how to name what you can see."

"Name what? I have no idea what you're talking about."

He absently ran his fingers over his own bracelet. "I know you can see it. The shadow on the land. The marks of its passing. It does move unseen. Until you cross the veil. All the signs have been revealed. Things are not right." He lifted a finger to silence her and tilted his head. "Listen."

She heard nothing but the muttering of men, the bottles clinking, the rumble of a truck passing by. She had no idea what he was talking about: shadows on the land, veils, unseen things. These were mad ramblings.

"Listen, beneath it all."

She heard nothing. Then, it was there for a moment. A child's cry in the breath of the wind that slipped through the door and as quickly as it had arisen then it was gone.

"Is that Maya? Where is she?" she asked.

"You would think I'm crazy."

She laughed. "Any more than I already do?"

"All of this." He swept his hands across the room, but she knew he was indicating much more than Western. "It's one place,

53

and then there is another place, and sometimes things from this other place come over. They cross the borderlands. They leave mangled bodies, scorches in the trees, hillsides collapse. Sometimes they want to gain a foothold here. And other times they are hungry. Sometimes they steal children."

"Maya is here. I got her back. She came out of the marsh."

"Something stepped out of the marsh. I agree with you there. Not Maya, though. She did not return, and you know that."

Jessie clenched her jaw to stop the trembling. She did not want to believe. She did not want to be dragged down this path.

Troy gulped the last of his beer, grabbed the full bottle she brought to the table, and stood. "I don't want to say this, but I have to. I have to be honest with you. Your daughter is gone and the other, the thing that is here in her place, will waste away. There is nothing for it to eat here. When it is gone, all hope is lost."

The words struck Jessie as if she had been punched in the belly. Her daughter could not be gone. She grabbed his wrist and jerked him back to his chair. "You're crazy. Absolutely mad. What did you do to my daughter?"

He did not resist. He sat back down.

"The thing is, Jessie, it's your fault. They only take those who aren't protected, those who are forgotten. They seek out those who are unloved, those who are a burden. They can sense that emptiness in your heart. Sniff it out like a shark after blood. You invited them in, whether you know it or not, and now it's done. Maya is gone. And this thing, this changeling, roosts in your house. It's an evil little thing, and soon it will waste away, but not before it tears your heart open, because if it has to suffer, it is going to make you suffer along with it. You had a beautiful child, a lovely girl, the dream of a future, brightness, and you could not get beyond only seeing yourself. The booze, the men, the selfishness. Maya is lost because of you."

Jessie made to grab at him again, but he pulled his arm back and stood. He hurried away from the table, and she wanted to rise with him, but she could not catch her breath. It felt as if everything drained out of her, as if she was stunned. When her energy finally returned, he was already out the door. She got up and ran after him, the men sitting at the bar tracking her with their desperate gazes, and when she yanked open the door, he was gone. The street empty. The wind shearing down the street, rattling store signs, paper and plastic racing along the curb.

Jessie wanted to run after him but he was gone.

11

THAT NIGHT, after Maya had been tucked into her bed, Jessie sat on the couch in the living room pretending to watch television, the volume turned low. She wanted to be numb. Too much had happened lately, and none of it made sense. She wanted everything to fade away, go back to dull normalcy, but what Troy had told her bothered her. It was unreal, but it had grabbed a hold of her. It explained so much.

Her mother puttered around the kitchen, gently banging pots and cleaning the dinner dishes, scrubbing the counter, before finally standing next to the couch, wiping her hands dry with a dish towel.

"I know you went to the Western. I know you went out drinking in the middle of the day while I was watching Maya. You can't be doing that."

"It's not like that. I had to talk to someone."

Her mother scoffed. "At a bar."

"You don't understand."

"I understand enough."

"You continually harp at me. I'm not doing anything wrong."

"You're not doing anything right. You're my daughter. I love you. You know that. And I know that deep down you love Maya, but you are too raw. You've got problems. The drinking, the drugs. You are messing up with your daughter. You lose her. You hit her. She's not eating. This is just wrong and you know it."

"It's more complicated than that."

"How is it more complicated than that? You tell me."

Jessie clenched her fists. She didn't know what to say. What Troy said was crazy, but it also made sense. It explained the changes in Maya. Her daughter had wandered off into the marsh and what returned was a changeling. That explained the roots in her hair, the smell, her lack of appetite, her biting Jessie. This wasn't her daughter. This was a thing.

But Jessie knew how absolutely insane all of that sounded. If she told her mother that, her mother would call the police. None of this should make any sense. This was crazy. Why the hell was she even believing any of what Troy had told her? That was absolute madness.

"I don't know," she finally said. "I don't know how to explain it. Have you noticed anything different about Maya? Hasn't she been acting strangely lately? Does she not seem like herself? Like maybe she is someone else? Do you think that maybe," she looked towards the bedroom, "that maybe, that is not Maya in there?"

Her mother's lower lip trembled. "You are scaring me, Jessie. I let you come back here because I thought you could get yourself back on your feet after all those drugs. I don't know anymore. You scare me. Can I even trust you with Maya? You know I found bruises on her arm. Like someone grabbed her too hard." Her mother let out a shuddering breath. "Jessie, I didn't want to do this but you've left me no choice. I've made a decision. I'm going to give you a couple of days, but then you need to leave, and Maya stays here. You need to go wherever it is that you need to go and get your head screwed on right. Clean up, detox, whatever it takes. It's just not safe anymore."

"I'm not leaving my daughter."

"You just told me that you don't think your daughter is your daughter. Do you not hear yourself talking?"

"You don't understand. She's been switched."

Tears streamed down her mother's cheeks. She did not even try to wipe them away. "You're sick, Jessie. You need to get help. Sheriff Reyes knows you hit Maya. A report was filed. He's sitting on it, as a favor to me. So we could talk. I can't have you around Maya like this. You are a danger to her. You're going to end up hurting her and I am not going stand by idly with that happens. She means too much to me. You either go away on your own or he will take you away. It's your choice."

"Neither of those are a choice."

"It's all you've got left, Jessie. You've painted yourself into this corner."

"Mom, please."

Her mother left the living room and Jessie sat alone, the empty sounds of the TV filling the room. She could not let it be left like that. She followed her mother back to her bedroom, but it was empty. She went to Maya's room and tried the door. It was locked. She knocked on it lightly. "Mom? Please."

Silence greeted her. Eventually Jessie went back to her room and pulled one of her bags out of the closet. She dug around until she found a small silver box. She popped the lid and took out a piece of paper folded into an envelope. She opened the paper and laid it flat on her bedside table. White powder sat on the paper. She quickly rolled a dollar bill and snorted it.

She let out a deep breath. The feeling would come soon. The pain and worry would vanish. She would have a little time of peace.

She licked her lips. She needed that numbness, the calm that would come. She needed to swim in that haze again. She needed something to get away from all this madness and slip into a place where all of that vanished, where her pain would be smothered, where pleasure rose again. She deserved that.

Jessie retreated to the bathroom. She turned on the faucet and soon steaming water thundered in the bottom of the tub. She took off her clothes. She was thinner than she remembered herself being, her face more drawn, her ribs showing, wrinkles all around her eyes.

She tested the water and lowered herself into the tub. The warmth, the euphoria, the steam washed over her.

She closed her eyes. How easy it was to drift somewhere else. The water, the white powder dream. She felt herself separating from her body, all the troubles, all the pain fading. She felt weightless and maybe if she just stayed here, she would eventually float away, her body disintegrating, any trace of her and her suffering in the world lost.

After a while she opened her eyes.

A layer of scum ringed the tub. Her mother had Maya in the bath earlier that evening, filling the tub with bubbles, scrubbing her skin red with a washcloth, desperate to get rid of that lingering smell.

She ran her finger over the scum. Oily black bits came away. She lifted her finger to her eyes. The black branched on her skin, slowly moving, following the prints of her skin as if seeking the lowest spot, as if seeking a cut and a way in.

She snatched a towel from the hook and wiped the blackness from her fingers. She stared at her body. She could see it. The black film settling on her. She shivered. It was if the scrabbling feet of thousands of insects crawled over her body. She stood quickly, catching the wall as her feet nearly slipped out from beneath her.

It itched. She scratched her arms, her belly, her thighs. She pulled the drain and turned the shower on full blast. Hot water scorched her. She soaped up a wash cloth and scrubbed, grinding against the itching, the itching that seeped beneath her skin, the itching that made her nerves suddenly light up with fire. She scrubbed until her skin turned red, scrubbed so hard in some spots that she rubbed her flesh raw. She needed to clean herself. She needed to get it off her skin. Soap, scalding water, the cloth. She scrubbed until the water pooling around her feet changed from gray to pink, and then finally she stopped, panting, bleeding, the fleeting feeling of euphoria gone, all hope of escape dashed.

She could not just run away.

12

Jessie showed up at the encampment in the last remnant of darkness before dawn.

She had run out of options. All the madness that Troy had claimed seemed real. The thing at her house was vicious, a beast, that had somehow been involved with the theft of her daughter. As crazy as what Troy had said, it all made sense. Nothing else fell into place. She was also running out of time. Her mother did not believe any of the things she said the fake Maya was doing, and had lost all faith in Jessie. If she did not leave the house, her mother would call the police.

She had not been able to sleep after the bath. She had felt the black oil clinging to her skin, even after she had scraped her skin raw. Something evil lived in that marsh, and it had taken her daughter.

Troy was her only hope to figure this out.

She pounded on the door of Troy's van until she heard him cursing inside. Finally, he slid open the door, a short machete in his hand. He shook his head and looked past her, at the other parked vehicles, and then to the campfire where a few men slept in sleeping bags on lawn chairs.

He wore a blanket wrapped around his shoulders, but otherwise he wore a thin t-shirt and boxer shorts. Tattoos decorated his bare legs and arms. Tibetan script and images of demons with swords covered his skin.

He blinked several times. She could smell the whiskey on his breath. She wondered if he could see the drugs lingering in her veins.

"You come pounding at this hour, you're lucky not to get a bullet in your gut."

"I need your help. How can I get Maya back?"

He winced as he straightened his spine. "Too early for this. Too late for that. You go away. I told you it's better at this point to just let things be. You keep poking at something, it might just come out of its hole and you don't want to face that down. Leave good enough alone already."

He started to slide the van door shut but Jessie stepped into the gap, blocking it with her body.

"I can't. It's my daughter. It's Maya. I see it now. Something's taken her. I want her back. I *need* her back."

He shook his head, closed his eyes, and cursed. "I can't help you."

"Please. I don't know what to do. Please!"

A headlamp turned on in one of the other cars. Figures moved in the shadows. A car door squealed open. "Troy? Everything all right over there?"

Troy muttered under his breath, stepped back, and motioned for Jessie to follow. After she stepped inside, he slid the door shut behind her.

He had modified the van for living, a built-in bed, bookshelves, a small space for a laptop computer. He switched on an overhead lamp. He cleared a stack of papers off a milk crate, brushed it with his hand, and indicated for her to sit. When he saw her scanning the titles of the books on the shelves, he spoke.

"Not your average Book of the Month Club collection. Like

I said before, I see myself as an amateur investigator and the things I am seeking are not what is apparent. One of these days, I'm going to write my own book, *The Book of Things Forgotten* or something like that. People claim we live in the Information Age, but we have truly forgotten more than we pretend to know."

"Can you help me get Maya back?"

He pulled a book from the shelf. It was leather-bound with gilded lettering. She smelled decay. He blew dust from the closed pages.

"The *Leksykon i antologia demonologi*. One of the few left in existence. The Nazis hoarded what copies they could. Most of them were lost in the final days of Berlin. The others were burned by the Church. Of course."

He thumbed through the book and when he found the page he was looking for her turned it around on his lap. He pointed to an illustration of a woman entangled in the limbs of a tree and reaching out for a young shepherd. The more Jessie looked at the drawing the more it changed. The woman was not entangled as much as it looked like she was one with the tree limbs, and while at first, it looked like she was reaching out for help, Jessie could now see that the woman was stretching out to seize the boy who seemed frozen in horror.

"The Dziwozona, a swamp demon, according to Slavic traditions. Legend claims the Dziwozona is an unwed mother who lost her child during birth. The mother is possessed by the swamp, becomes one with the evil that lurks there. All the vile things gather, the mud, the roots, the slime. They gather around that shunned woman, roiling with her rage, until she and the evil are one, all of the humanity drained from her until all that remains is a tangle of evil, hungry, waiting. When the time is right, the demon breaks through the veil between worlds and steals an unloved child."

"I loved her. I did. I said those things, but I loved her."

"I'm not here to judge," he said. "But the demon did what its nature demands."

"There's no such thing as a demon."

"Maybe not in the way people think. Like some grinning, horned red devil. That's the cultural lens, a way to try to explain the unexplainable. But this thing exists."

Jessie pointed to the illustration in the book. "Is this what has Maya? This woman."

"It does not look like this. A lovely maiden entangled in roots. There is no woman anymore. Don't you understand? We create these folktales, these legends, to make sense of that which we can't even begin to understand. We are so desperate to reduce everything to pieces so we can digest it. But the demon is born from suffering, a woman who lost her child, but it is no longer the woman that remains. She becomes so consumed by her loss that she becomes that loss. All that pain transformed. Sorrow embodied. And her only way to feed that desperation is to find an unloved child. But what is it anymore? It is no longer a woman. It dissolves into lonely places. A whispering wind. A sudden chill. Black sucking mud."

"Can we get Maya back?"

He ran his fingers over his books. "Everything written in here is words on the wind. This book says you can take the changeling and beat it with willow branches. Another book says to heat the changeling in an oven or drown it in bracken water and its fear will bring its mother out from hiding. Another says to push them through standing stones."

"So what do we do?"

"There's no operating manual or guidebook for all this."

"You'll help me?"

"I'm not the best person for this. I'm old. I'm tired. A bit of a drunk. I'm no hero."

She grabbed at his sleeve. "But you know about these things. You've fought against demons before."

"I'm the wrong person for this."

"I have no one else to help me."

He swallowed back words and frowned.

"Please," she said.

He found a whiskey bottle, unscrewed the lid, and choked down a shot. "I shouldn't be saying this. But I will do it. I will help. But be warned. We can't just walk her back you know. Everything has a price."

"I'm willing to pay the price. Anything to get her back. Anything to erase this nightmare."

13

"One last day," Jessie said to her mother in the kitchen the next morning. "Then I'll go. I'll get clean. I just want one more day with Maya."

Her mother had agreed, colorless lips pursed. When the sound of the truck faded, Jessie called Troy. It was safe now. Her mother had gone to work. He could come over. They could go into the swamp. They could get Maya back.

"Put on a jacket," Jessie said. Maya, or the changeling, whatever it was, sat on the couch, still dressed in pajamas, the blue pajamas with the bear faces on them that Jessie had bought her daughter last Christmas.

"I'm hungry." Maya balled up the belly of her pajamas in her fist.

"You didn't eat anything again. That's why you're hungry, you little monster. Put on a jacket."

As the words slipped out of her mouth, Jessie regretted saying them. Maya's eyes edged in tears and she looked so small. This was madness. What was she doing? That was Maya sitting on the couch. Her own daughter. She was hungry. She was suffering.

There was no such thing as changelings. She began to wonder if Troy was mad and she was being dragged into his vortex.

But she could not forget everything that had happened. The biting, the black blood, the roots in her hair. She had seen those things.

She thought about the black oil in the tub. But could she trust herself? When she had felt that on her skin she had been high. Maybe there had been no black oil. When she had first heard the voice on the wind, it was just after she had snorted coke and was half drunk.

Jessie went into the bedroom and packed a small bag with clean clothes and another jacket for Maya. She sat on the bed and grabbed her head.

What if she was imagining this? What if she was seeing things? Could she be hallucinating? Her mother had not seen any of these things. Hearing voices, seeing things, imagining her daughter had turned into a monster.

But Troy reaffirmed everything. He had been the one who had tested her skin with the cross. He had shown her the image of the swamp demon from the book. He said these horrible creatures of the imagination existed.

Could she trust Troy? The man lived in a van. He talked about demons and witches, about other worlds, and changelings as easily as another person talked about the weather or vegetables at the market. He was as damaged as Jessie, addicted, stinking of booze and weed, apart from others. She thought back to the day that Maya had disappeared and the questions that the police asked about Troy. Why would he be a suspect? How would he even know where to lead the police? What didn't she know about him?

Jessie let out several shuddering breaths, then returned to the living room.

Maya-not-Maya had still not put on a jacket. She peered over the back of the couch. "Can we get something to eat, Mommy?"

"Later. We're going for a walk first."

"I'm cold."

Tires rolled over the gravel driveway. Looking through the window, Jessie watched Troy's van pulled up behind the barn, coming to a stop, hidden from the road.

Jessie slipped the bag over her shoulder and grabbed Maya by the wrist.

The morning air was biting, colder than it should have been. It constricted her lungs, shortening her breath. Jessie curled her fingers into her palms and hunched her shoulders.

They found Troy behind the barn, staring over the fence into the marsh. A layer of fog blanketed the grasses and the distant bay, fingers of mist extending through the tree-lined ridge on the opposite side. The reds and browns of the marsh grasses disintegrated into the white of the fog. The black mirror surface of the middle of the bay was lost.

"I'm cold. I want something to eat."

"Ignore the changeling," said Troy. "And you need to hold onto it. It will try to run." He had strapped a machete to a belt around his waist.

"Do I need something too?" asked Jessie. "We have guns in the house."

"Just courage, kid. This won't be easy." He lifted a loop of wire on the fence, opened a gap, then stepped through.

Jessie tightened her grip on Maya's wrist. It felt as cold as stone. Her arm trembled in Jessie's hand. Maya pulled back. "I don't want to go in there again. Please."

"We're just going for a walk."

As they entered the marsh, the fog began to eat everything.

With a minute the distances closed, fog pressing in from all sides, and Troy, walking only a few steps ahead, became a ghost leading them through a maze of grasses. Jessie glanced over her shoulder and the barn had faded behind a screen of mist. The trees on the ridge on the opposite side of the bay blended into a gray mass.

The wetness of the fog layered on Jessie's hoodie and she wished she had worn something heavier. Already a chill was settling into her.

She tried to follow Troy closely, to match his steps, but the ground was uneven, black pools of water cutting across the trail, and worse, Maya kept pulling as if she wanted to run off. Jessie tottered, steps uncertain, trying to avoid the slippery mud and the water but soon her shoes were sopping, her socks heavy, and cold pain needled her feet.

"Mommy, I want to go home."

Jessie focused on the path ahead. She refused to get distracted by the changeling, the creature that pretended to be her daughter.

As they pushed deeper into the marsh, sound became muffled. While she heard the splash of her feet and the squelching of her steps, it was as if she was hearing someone else walking away from her, each step more distant, fading. The trilling of morning birds eroded into an insectile buzz.

She plunged ahead, gaze drifting from the silhouette of Troy to where to place her next step, to Maya squirming beneath her grip.

When she looked up again, Troy was gone. She stared at the white shadows. Shapes shifted, darkness buckled. She could discern clumps of grasses and fetid pools maybe two body lengths away but everything beyond that had disintegrated into whiteness.

"Troy, where are you? I've lost you. Troy?"

A waft of rot clotted her sinuses. She coughed, held her breath. She had found dead animals before, rats in the crawl-spaces above her Portland apartment, bloated, maggot-filled, seeping, and this odor was that and it smelled not of a single rat, but of thousands. She gagged, fighting the bile that rose.

She sputtered and plunged forward, wet grasses clinging to her legs, her pants soaked.

A shadow rose up before her and she stepped back, her foot

sliding out beneath her. She fell into sopping grasses pulling Maya with her.

"I told you to stay close." Troy's face gathered form as he leaned in.

"This fog."

"Of course, it does not want us to find it. It does not want us to find its den. The Dziwozona knows."

"Maybe we should turn back."

Troy pulled a flask from his jacket, unscrewed the cap, and took a swig. He then extended it to Jessie.

"What is that?"

"Liquid courage. And maybe something a little stronger."

The whiskey seared the back of her throat but it helped. It warmed her. It masked the stench of rot. It loosened the fear that had clawed into her skin. She took another gulp and then handed the flask back to him. The dullness was welcoming.

"The thing is though," he continued, "we might have a little problem."

"What are you talking about?"

"I don't know where we're going."

"To find this thing."

"But I don't where it is. It's here somewhere. I thought it would be obvious, that something would guide us towards it. I can't find any signs."

"So you're just taking us for a stroll in the marsh? Great way to stretch the legs, get some exercise. Are we just walking in circles? You drunken idiot, do you really know anything? Anything at all? Or are you just making all of this up from the books you read? Have you ever seen one of these things?"

"A Dziwozona is a creature of legend. They are rare. Again, that's only the name that we have given it. It is a being that has crossed the membrane. Our words cannot even describe the other world."

Maya tore at Jessie's sleeve. "I'm cold." Her teeth chattered. "I want to go home. Mommy, please."

Troy pointed at Maya. "Don't listen to it. It fills your head with untruths. It feeds off your connection with your daughter. It'll do anything it can to turn you back from finding your daughter. We must be getting close."

Jessie laughed. "To what? You don't even know where we're going or what this thing is, if it even exists at all. When Maya disappeared, why was Sheriff Reyes asking about you? Why was he sending someone over to check in on you?"

"This is more of her getting inside your head. I'm warning you."

"Tell me why Reyes was asking about you."

"Outside of Lawrence, Kansas. Something tore a gap in the border between worlds. It wanted teenage girls. It drank their vitality and then dumped them in the river. I tracked it down into the heart of a bramble, stepped across that border. Too late for those girls. But I sealed that breech. There is a price for everything. They found me on the banks of the river, naked, and I told them it was all over, but they wanted a scapegoat. They tried to pin those dead girls on me. Reyes knows. He thinks I have secrets. I do. They just aren't the ones that he imagines. They're so much worse."

"I'm turning back. I can't do this. This is crazy. There is no other world. There are no demons in the swamp. This is Maya. I'm losing my shit. I need to get away. I need to get my head on straight. I have to figure out how to be a good mother."

Troy grabbed her arm, his hand trembling. "If you turn back now, you'll lose your real daughter forever."

"I can't do this."

She tightened her grip on Maya and began marching back in what she thought was the direction that she came. The fog was less dense to the right and she figured that might be the way out. Troy called after her but she ignored him. He was crazy. He was leading her into a deeper hell than any that she had created for herself. She walked away, leaving him behind.

"Thank you, Mommy, thank you."

"I'll get you back home. I'll get all of this figured out. When I come back, I'll be the mommy you were supposed to have. I'll never leave you, Maya."

That's when she heard the shriek, distant like a hawk floating on thermals, and she froze in her steps.

"Let's keep going, Mommy."

She strained to hear it again but the shriek was singular, and it vanished to a fading echo, a memory disintegrating in her skull. But she knew what it was. It was Maya, the true Maya, calling for her, calling for her mother.

Jessie turned. The fog swirled thick, moisture visible, the distances swallowed. But even so, she could see what had not been visible before.

A path lay before her. A path of crushed grasses, fetid pools, and trailing slime. Something gargantuan had slithered through this grass, the thing that had stolen her child.

She stared at the trail in the grasses, knowing without doubt that it would lead to her daughter. She could no longer turn back towards her home. She needed to follow this path and towards whatever had created it. It was the only way to bring the real Maya home.

14

LATER, Jessie found the hole in the ground.

She had followed that furrowed path, climbing over slippery mounds, wading through knee-deep water, fighting grass that snagged her limbs, all the while never releasing her grip on the other Maya. She led the way. Troy trailed behind her, no longer confident, mumbling to himself, unable to see the depression in grasses, the obvious trail of slime. With each step, the stench rose. The rot of sodden vegetables, an animal corpse in the walls, the sickening sweet smell of flowers from a promised spring that might never come. Troy could not smell that, either. He had no sense of where she led. But he followed. Because he believed.

The other Maya followed too. But only because she was dragged along, whimpering, crying, begging. She could not keep her feet beneath her, so she was pulled along. One shoe had fallen off, her bare foot blue, puckered with the water.

"Home," she cried.

Jessie steeled herself. She would not give in. She had heard the cries of Maya. She knew what was real. This changeling, this replacement she towed along, was not real. It was a creature. Demon spawn. Its very existence in Nova Albion, in the marsh, in this world, meant that there was no space for the real Maya, Jessie's flesh and blood. Jessie needed to get rid of the changeling to get her daughter back.

Jessie ignored the triggered emotions from the wailing creature at her side. The other Maya sounded so much like the real Maya. It tore at her heart. She choked down the pain. She had to ignore all of that. Her hand was so cold it cramped. The icy wind burned her lips. Her feet so sodden and numb, she could barely feel the shape of the ground.

She turned her thoughts away from the pain and the suffering and, most of all, the doubt and focused on the trail through the grasses and the mud, the path through the thorns and deep water.

Time curled on itself. Minutes melted into hours, into days, into minutes again. She pushed on. She had heard the cry of Maya, the real Maya. She could not give up now.

She waded into a particularly vile pool, waist deep. Cold sent daggers into her thighs, invisible hands of mud grasped beneath the surface. Every step was a hard-fought battle. Halfway across the pool, the other Maya disappeared under the waters. Her arm, slippery like a fish, slid through Jessie's grasp. But she tightened it at the last minute at her wrist and jerked her back to the surface.

Jessie fought back tears. Her knees ached. She could not stop shivering from the cold that settled into her muscles. She pushed on, finally reaching the opposite bank, and dragged herself and the other Maya up a ramp of mud and slime, sliding back as much as she was climbing.

She grasped a vine to pull herself out of the frigid waters. She yelped. A thorn pierced her palm and even though burning pain lit her hand, she refused to let go. Maya was counting on her. Step by step, she hauled herself and the changeling out of the pool and onto a small island surrounded by oily black water.

When she reached flat ground, she let go of the vine. A drop of dark blood glistened on the vine and then she watched in horror as the drop was drawn into the thumb-sized thorn. She tracked the vine back towards a tangled blackberry bramble rising on the center of the island.

Something had crashed through the center of the blackberry patch, crushing the canes with its weight, something that had no fear of the thorns. Maybe something that felt no pain. An opening had been hollowed in the patch. This was where the path led.

Jessie blinked back tears. She had found her path back to Maya. She wanted to scream in triumph at the sky, for her voice to burn away the fog. But at the same time she was filled with doubt and fear. Reality had turned into a nightmare, one that felt as if it had no end.

In the heart of the blackberry patch, earth, raw and broken, piled around a hole, a hole as round as Jessie was tall, a hole that descended steeply into blackness.

The stench of rot coursed out of the hole, and Jessie vomited, whiskey and bile burning her throat and nose. She fell to her knees, suddenly light headed, her bloodied hand steadying her.

Troy stood next to her, hands on knees, a long string of saliva hanging from his lips. He struggled to breath, the air raspy and crackling as he inhaled. "The den of the Dziwozona."

He had headlamps and he gave one to Jessie.

"It breathes," said Troy.

"It can't breathe. It's a hole." Even as she said that, Jessie had her doubts. Fetid air coursed out of the hole, lifting its crown of dead grasses. She blinked, eyes watering from the unnatural wind. "Listen. It's her."

Behind the humming of air, she heard Maya, voice unintelligible as if she no longer could remember how to form words, as if she were disintegrating in that hole in the ground.

Suddenly, the air stopped pulsing, the grasses fell flat, and the echo of Maya's voice vanished.

Jessie felt like bursting into tears. She wanted to turn back.

All of this was madness and getting madder. But she had heard Maya's voice. She could not abandon her.

She looked at Troy. He tottered. "How deep do we have to go?"

"Ask the changeling."

Jessie dropped to her knees and shook the other Maya. "Tell me what I need to know. What is in there? Is Maya still alive?"

"Mommy, I want to go home."

Jessie slapped the changeling across the face. "Stop your lies, you dirty little bitch." She slapped her over and over until Troy caught her by the wrist.

"You don't need to do this. She was born for this. She knows no better."

Maya cowered on her knees, fingers clenching the muddy earth. "Mommy."

"I know, I know, you want to go home. You are going to go home, back to whatever monster you were spawned from, and I'll get my Maya back."

"I don't want to go."

"You have no choice." She turned to Troy. He looked old, suddenly, any vulpine features lost. He hugged himself in a failed effort to stop shivering. She realized she could not rely on him to do what she knew had to be done. She'd be lucky for him to even be able to follow. She was the one who would need to rescue Maya.

"I'll go down first, then the changeling, and you come last. You make sure she stays in between us. Can you do that, Troy?"

As Jessie edged towards the hole, she clicked on the headlamp. Cold air touched her skin. The disturbed earth was soft, full of wriggling worms and shiny black beetles. She sank up to her ankles in the soil, and as she got closer to the lip, her feet slid on the upturned soil. She gasped, muscles tightening, afraid that she would suddenly tumble into the pit.

She steadied her breath and inched forward until she could shine her light down the hole.

The tunnel dropped straight down into blackness. She wished they had brought a rope. She angled her head to the sides of the opening. The light picked up ridges of compacted dirt lining the interior of the tunnel. Almost like the rungs of a ladder built into the wall of earth. She could step on the ridges, climbing down, just praying that they would hold her weight. She played the light down the walls following them until the light dissipated. She could not see the bottom. If there was one.

She turned to Troy whose only answer was a grim nod. He too had been staring down into the depths of the tunnel. Again, he waited for her to decide what to do.

Jessie began her descent. She turned around, got down on her hands and knees, and backed over the edge, a small stream of soil draining into the hole with her. She lowered one foot over the edge, scraping around blindly. She could not find the first ridge. She backed up a bit more. The dirt beneath her suddenly collapsed and she began to slide. She clawed the ground but still she was pulled along. Right as she was about to scream to Troy for help, her foot landed solidly on the ridge of soil. Her weight held. She stopped falling. When her breath and heart slowed, she continued her descent, feet and hands finding and testing the rings on the wall before she shifted her weight.

She descended about ten feet before she found the first ledge.

"Send Maya down."

Maya came next, and then Troy, all of them crowded on the ledge, pressed against the walls of glistening mud and stone. They repeated this four more times before the tunnel bottomed out into a cavernous chamber, thirty feet high and thirty feet wide. It did not look natural. It looked excavated. A passage had been dug through one of the walls.

They turned their lights into it. It led into blackness.

"We keep going?" asked Troy.

"Is there any other choice at this point?"

Jessie was forced to stoop over to enter the tunnel. She immediately felt the strain in her hamstrings and a dull ache in her back. But even so, it was better than the blind descent they had just overcome.

Jessie's headlamp lit up a fine mist that clouded the tunnel. It gave a sense that the space in front of her was shortened, as if the walls slowly closed in, and she were being forced into ever tighter passages. The descent had filled her with the fear of a bottomless pit, of falling to her death. This was the opposite. This was smothering.

It was not just her perception that the walls were closing in. They actually were. The passage narrowed as if whatever had burrowed this hole shrank in size. The walls pressed in on her shoulders. The ceiling dropped. She had to crouch even lower to avoid touching the mud and stone, and most of all, the glistening mucus that dripped from the ceiling and walls. It was hard work. Her thighs burned. The small of her back tightened, muscles quivering.

As she marched forward, the walls changed, the dirt and stone giving way to pink, tumorous flesh, as if they traveled through the intestine of some giant beast.

Fear washed over her. The fleshy walls appeared to pulse. She imagined them suddenly constricting, flattening her to the ground, pinning her arms until she would be stuck there, squeezing her, digesting her, acids eating away at skin, muscle, and then bone.

Finally the passage ballooned and they found themselves standing in a bulbous chamber. Jessie turned her head, the lamp lighting the walls and the ceiling. Funnels of gray fungi dripped from the ceiling. The fleshy walls quivered. She let the light rest on a pile white stones stacked in the rough shape of a pyramid in the center of the chamber.

As she stared at the pyramid, she began to see shapes: eye sockets, jawbones, teeth.

"What is this?" she asked. "What the hell?"

Troy squatted next to the pile. He extended his hand and then withdrew it to his chest. "Children. These bones."

Jessie reached out to steady herself, feeling as if the room was spinning into a vortex around the pile of bones, but there was nothing on which to anchor and she collapsed to her knees.

She touched a skull that was so cold it sent shivers up her spine. Was one of these Maya's? She clenched her jaw fighting the urge to scream.

Something flashed in the corner of her eye, a shape visible, and then vanishing back up the tunnel.

"The changeling!" screamed Troy. "It's getting away."

15

JESSIE RACED AFTER THE CHANGELING, back through the tunnel and toward the surface. She bumped her head, brushed her arms and hands against the fleshy walls, fought the feeling of the walls collapsing in and swallowing her. When she reached the chamber, she caught sight of the changeling clambering up and over the edge, escaping.

Jessie looked over her shoulder. She had sprinted out of the room of bones, leaving Troy behind. She waited for a moment, expecting him to come after to her and help her capture the changeling, but the passage behind was silent. He had not followed. She was on her.

Without waiting any longer, she scaled the wall back towards the surface.

Soon she emerged back into the gloomy marsh. She knew she had to keep going to get Maya back. But a wave of exhaustion washed over her. She fell to her knees.

All of this was madness. Her daughter being replaced by a changeling. The hidden world of the marsh. The tunnel beneath the ground. She closed her eyes and covered her ears, wishing all of this was a hallucination, but when she opened her eyes again, nothing had changed.

She wanted to stay there, and curl into the bushes, and wait until someone found her, a rescuer, someone to pull her out of this morass and out of the life that she had created for herself. Even if all of this was real and even if she rescued her daughter, what lay ahead for her? More nights with strangers in bars, her mother harping on every single thing that she did, the comfortable numbness of drink and drugs? Where was the grand life that she was supposed to live? Where was the family, the laughter, the brightness?

The cold, muddy water seeped through her pants, sending icy needles of pain into her knees. She hugged herself and shivered against the pressing fog.

She could not just stay here. She could not simply do nothing. Because if she did, she would die, the changeling would escape, and Maya would die. Maybe she was already dead in that pile of bones.

Jessie screamed.

The changeling was racing back to the house. It wanted to wear the skin of Maya's life, even as it wasted away. It would eat away at whatever little happiness remained to Jessie.

She would not let it.

She staggered to her feet, and ran, not even knowing where she was going. One direction seemed to be the same as the other, the mounds of dead grasses and pools of black water in all directions.

But then she caught a glimpse of where the fog thinned, where pale light shone even if only slightly brighter in the gloom that sealed her in.

She loped off towards the light, lungs aching, thighs burning, tears distorting her vision.

Eventually, in the dissipating fog, she saw the changeling, small, stumbling, splashing through the dank pools. Jessie charged ahead propelled by a growing anger. Her large strides carried her.

She caught the changeling before it broke out of the fog and crossed back to the other side. She crushed it into her arms. The changeling squirmed and Jessie could barely hang on, its skin slick and oily like a fish; its flesh as cold as death.

It still wore the mask of Maya, the blonde hair, the plump lips, and it carried her voice. "Mommy, let me go. Let me go back home. Why are you so mad at me?"

Jessie squeezed harder, vising the creature's arm.

"You're not going to run away again, you little demon."

The changeling had no answers and broke down in tears, sucking in fluttering mouthfuls of air.

Jessie fought a surge of emotion. This creature looked so much like her daughter. She imagined it deceiving everyone else, but she would not let it fool her. It would sit on that couch, wrapped in blankets and cooing and getting everything it wanted, all the while eating away at the world while the real Maya died in that pit, slowly digested into a pile of white bones.

"We're going back. I'm taking you back and getting Maya."

She heard a voice cut through the gloom.

"Jessie! Where are you?"

She looked up from the changeling. The fog had melted away to a hazy membrane, and on the other side she could distinguish the shapes of the world, the blocks of the house and the barn, the roll of the distant ridge, the silhouette of her mother standing on the opposite side of the membrane. The mists flashed red and blue, and Jessie saw Reyes's police cruiser. They were assembling another search party.

The changeling screamed out for help.

Jessie's mother stepped forward and her face sharpened. The membrane stretched with her, thinning, as if at any moment, it might snap and she would break through to this other world.

But that was what the changeling wanted. It wanted to be

rescued again. It wanted to be brought back into the world where it could occupy the space that Maya was supposed to inhabit.

"Maya, sweetie, where are you?"

Jessie clamped a hand over the changeling's mouth. It bit her and screamed.

Jessie's mother took another step forward, the membrane stretching into visible strands.

Jessie grabbed the back of the changeling's head, fingers intertwined in her hair, and shoved her face first into the mud. It fought hard, arms flailing, legs kicking, body bucking, but Jessie held tight, pressing harder to mute the keening from the creature's mouth.

"Maya?" Her mother held there, uncertain. "I thought I heard something, a voice calling for help."

Reyes stood behind her, a gray silhouette, and said something in response, his words an unintelligible hum.

"I'm sure I did." Then her mother stepped back, and the border between the worlds thickened. The flashing lights dimmed and the silhouettes of the other world blended into a dull glow that gradually darkened.

Jessie waited until the fog was uniform around her, the directions of the world lost to her, and then she released her grip.

"You're coming back now," she said to the changeling beneath her.

But it did not answer. It did not move.

She rolled it onto its back.

The other Maya no longer breathed, thick gray clay plugging its nostrils, teeth painted with the sticky mud. Its bloodshot eyes, dull, all glow of stolen life gone, stared past Jessie, beyond the realm of gloom.

Jessie gathered the body in her arms, hugging the small bundle to her chest, and turned back towards the darkness, to find the tunnel again, to bring her daughter home.

16

THE CORPSE WEIGHED HEAVILY in Jessie's arms. An icy stone against her heaving chest. She should not have been crying as she plunged back towards the tunnel because this creature in her arms was not her daughter, not her flesh and blood. It was a monster born of muck and despair. It was the spawn of a swamp demon, an abomination that tried to steal from her. But, even so, it wore the mask of Maya, in life and in death, and Jessie could not turn her heart from it.

The corpse felt like a bag of ice in her arms. The cold seeped through Jessie's shirt. It penetrated to her skin, like slowly unraveling frozen veins, and its icy roots dug deeper, through skin, through bone, searing muscle, all the way to her heart. Jessie screamed. She suddenly did not know if the world was what she thought it was. Had she made a mistake? Had she killed her own daughter?

She stopped, knees locked, and wiped at the mud from the face of the little being in her arms. Maya's cheeks, Maya's lips, her eyes staring blindly towards the heavens. This was her daughter. It was not some changeling. These things did not exist. All that existed was pain, and a reality shaped by drink, and drugs, and delusion. She did not know. She did not know anything anymore.

Jessie staggered onwards, through swirling mists, through a world that could not really exist, a world of nightmares. Her feet were sinking into puddles that formed pools and she fell to her hip nearly dropping Maya as she crumpled to the sodden ground. She lay there, wheezing, the sky a swirl of dark threaded clouds.

She waited, desperate for things to right themselves as the clouds shifted, darkened, oily stripes pulling across the heavens. The wind picked up. Vicious. Battering. The grasses hissed in response and she bent to them trying to understand the whispers that unfurled beneath the surface. She could almost make out the words. Hard ticks, sibilance, popping. What was she being told?

She squeezed the cold corpse against her chest. She wanted it to twitch, to spit the mud out, to suddenly burst back to life. She remembered that first day in the hospital bed when she held Maya, after a long night of pain, of anguish and torn flesh that transported her to the edge of another world, the sudden wash of euphoria as she held the babe in her arms, Paul, with that half smile, the smile that she always thought lit up only for her until she realized that it did not, maybe it never did. Maybe it smiled only for him, for some secret that he was never willing to reveal.

He had opened worlds to her. Love, family, and then all the seductive children of the poppy. That last world was the one that always loved her back. The one that never betrayed her. The one that melted all the troubles of her world away. It never screamed, or pissed its pants, or bit her. It did not keep her up at night with its crying. It never asked anything of her.

Lying there in the swamp mud, she thought about never moving again. She imagined the clouds swirling light, dark, light again. Days passing. The hazy ball of the sun marking time across the sky. She would settle into the swampy ground, still. Her skin would pucker and swell, redden with sores, pus, bleeding. Her cheeks would thin, her lips crack, skin slowly slough off. Black flies would land on her, kissing her lips, her eyelids, bite, laying eggs. Her flesh would rot and the grasses would grow into her. Until nothing remained but bones, the bones of a mother and her child, or it would be the bones of a woman and the skeleton of a horned demon, or the bones of a demon puppet made of wood, flesh from packed mud, hair of lifeless grasses.

Here, in the cold mud, she could fade away from the world. No need for the milk of the poppy. Here, she could close her eyes and let the fog and the marsh consume her. She could become one with everything, all pain, all regret, all dashed hopes gone, disintegrated, recycled back into stagnant water, bunch grasses, and droplets of mist. Maybe a single flower would rise from where she fell. Would that not be the perfect life?

She was almost there, lured by the song of the swamp, ready to let the grasses entangle her and swallow her deep into the earth when she heard the voice beckoning beneath the wind.

Maya! She lived.

Jessie pushed herself to sitting.

She heard it again, a low plaintive cry, a sound that connected to Jessie's soul, that cut through all other noise and arrowed straight to her heart. *Maya! My daughter!*

She unfolded to standing, arms still clinging to the corpse. Her legs trembled. Her breath was heavy. She should have collapsed. She should have given up. She had nothing left. All of this madness and pursuit, and she was dead tired now.

But Maya called and Jessie, choosing to be a mother, stumbled towards the voice, towards the tunnel in the earth, towards the pile of bones, towards that beacon of hope.

17

She found Troy in the chamber of bones. When she emerged again through the tunnel, he looked up suddenly. He had never left the room.

"Jessie, you're here. I thought you were never coming back. I had drifted off. I was dreaming of seeds and tendrils, of stretching through the soil. I swore I was sprouting roots. This place is dangerous. It lures you in. I was almost ready." He wiped the tears from his eyes with the backs of his wrists. He fixed his gaze on the body in her arms. He winced. "You caught the changeling. Let's finish this horrid affair."

"It's dead." She laid the changeling on the ground. She could not look at it. It was Maya.

"No, no, no. This can't be. It must be playing a trick on us." He stood up and turned the other Maya's head back and forth. He wiped at the mud. "What did you do?"

"We were at the border between the worlds. She was calling for my mother. They were there, on the other side. We would have been found. I had to make her be quiet. I had to stop the screams. I never would have been able to come back. They would have taken me away. Maya would be lost forever."

"You can't kill the changeling. It doesn't work like that."

"How does it work then?"

"I don't know but it can't work like that."

"You don't really know anything, do you? You read your books and fill my head with ideas but you have no idea what any of this is. Do you even know what you're leading us towards? Are we even going to be able to get out of here? Look at all these bones. It eats children. Is Maya even alive anymore?"

Troy could not look at the bones. He gnawed his lower lip. He was muddy, his clothes sodden, the lines in his face more drawn. He could have been old enough to be Jessie's father. "We press on. We can't turn back now. If there is any hope of a single child being alive, we need to press on."

"And kill this thing?" asked Jessie.

"Kill it? How do we kill it?" He threw his hands in the air, shaking his head.

"There's nothing in your book about this swamp demon, nothing about how to kill it, or release it from its curse?"

"Nothing you'll find in any of those books is prescriptive. The words are guideposts. What is a demon? A word we created to describe the unexplained. That's the curse of humans. We are always trying to understand and make order of the world, but it is not built on order. It is built on chaos, on disintegration. Everything moves from order to disorder, dispersing, eroding despite all our attempts to pretend that somehow things are getting better, that somehow, we will live forever. Everything falls apart. Everything decays. Order is the dream. Chaos is what we live."

"You're useless. You know that, don't you?"

"I got us this far."

She laughed. "Lost in a swamp that does not exist. In the fucking intestine of some beast staring at the bones of devoured children. You certainly got us somewhere."

He looked past the bones to where the tunnel continued and out of which a hot breath of air coursed. "One way to go."

"Straight into the belly of hell, I suppose."

"We'll find Maya."

Jessie prodded the bones with her foot. "Or will get eaten. Either way, all of this will end. Chaos or not."

She bent and picked up the changeling. She shuffled forward, deeper into the tunnel, the life she knew disappearing behind her. Troy lumbered after her.

The walls of the tunnel constricted even further, and soon Jessie was crawling, one hand clutching the changeling to her chest. She had to stop often, switching arms. Troy offered to carry it for a while but she refused. This was her burden. This was the price that she needed to pay for the days when she slept off a hangover, parked the kid in front of the television, slipped out to the bar instead of tucking her baby in for the night. Only she could make this right.

The air thickened, heavy with hot moisture, and when Jessie stopped, she gasped, trying to draw in enough air to fight the growing feeling of light-headedness. She knew she could not stop for too long because if she did, she feared she would lie down and give up all hope.

As she moved deeper, the tunnel changed. The mud and stone sloughing off until the walls were white, fleshy, and she could not help but feel that she crawled through an intestine, her hands and feet sinking into the yielding surface. She shivered each time the surface beneath her wiggled in a spasm. Fear burst free inside her. She waited for the walls to suddenly contract and to be swallowed down towards a stomach gurgling in acids and half-digested children.

Instead a wall appeared ahead, white, swirling. Black flecks flew out of it. She could not imagine what blocked their passage.

As she got closer, her headlight flashed across a scene of horror. The wall was alive, a door of squirming maggots, and black flies roiled out of it, shooting down the tunnel, bouncing off her lips, buzzing in her hair.

"We need to keep going," said Troy.

"I can't. This is too much. No."

"Can we even turn back now?"

She was not sure whether he meant because the tunnel had narrowed to a sleeve or because they had come so far.

"This is a fucking nightmare. I just want to die," she said.

"We have to be close. With this in front of us, what could be worse?"

She laughed. The sound was shrill, and it took great effort to calm herself. "What if this never ends? What if it is one horror after another?"

"If we turn around, we will never come back. You will be arrested, locked up somewhere. Maya will be lost. You know that, right? Are you ready to give up your daughter forever?"

"It shouldn't be this hard. It shouldn't be this much of a struggle. Why couldn't I have been given an easy, happy life? Why is there so much pain?"

"You have to make a choice, Jessie."

She took a deep breath, held onto the image of Maya, and then plunged through the wall of maggots.

18

PASSING through the wall of maggots, Jessie thought she would die. She plunged into the stench of rotting flesh, the maggots squirming, wiggling at her eyes, and she wanted to scream. She wanted to let the terror escape but to do so would mean opening her mouth to the mass of flesh eaters. She pushed through, swimming in the wall, and just when she thought there was no end, that she would be forever trapped, that her mind would finally break, she tumbled through.

She spat and gasped. She tossed the corpse from her. She swiped at her arms, smacking the maggots off her skin. She snorted them out of her nose. They tangled in her hair. Her body trembled and she let out a low wail.

She could feel them on her skin, under her skin, sliding through her veins. She scratched and tore. She leapt away from the wall, arms flailing, legs stomping.

"They're gone," said Troy. He grabbed her hands and held them to his chest.

"The maggots! I can feel them crawling."

"Jessie, open your eyes."

She reluctantly opened her eyes, eyes that she thought were

already open. The maggots were completely gone. Her arms were streaked red from her own fingernails. Clumps of her hair tangled between her fingers. She tasted the copper of blood in her teeth.

Troy stared past her. She followed his gaze.

They stood in a chamber of flesh and plants. The walls were pink, glistening, tumescent, pulsing with veins and raised scars. From these scars, roots and pale white tendrils stretched out, strange bulbs, polyps or fruit, hanging from them. The air smelled different, too. A heady sweetness mixed with damp rot. She was reminded of being deep in an untraveled forest, a place where life and death mixed comfortably.

In the center of the chamber, a tangle of root and flesh grew. She could not see where plant ended and flesh began. Tendrils poking out from the mass swayed as if they sensed and sought Jessie and Troy.

Something moved in the center of the tangle. Tiny fingers. Lips opening and closing.

Maya.

"I don't want this anymore," said Jessie. "I want all of this to end."

"She's here. Get her and let's be done with the demon."

Jessie crumpled to her knees in front of the tangle. "Maya, my sweet."

She bent forward. The tendrils tracked her movement, cold white plant flesh touching and tasting her skin. She shuddered at the contact. She could sense the hunger of the tangle.

She thrust her hands deeper, parting leafy growth and distorted cancerous flesh, until she touched Maya. Her child's eyes fluttered, waking briefly from a dream state before falling again into a stupor. Jessie choked back tears and then wrapped her fingers gently around her daughter's back and pulled.

Maya did not break free. Jessie tried again, pulling harder. After a third time, she cleared the leaves back to see why she might be stuck. Tendrils had rooted into her daughter, entwined her limbs, and held her captive.

"Give it the changeling," said Troy. "One for one. It needs something. Give it what it gave us."

Jessie did not want to let go of her daughter. She was afraid that if she did, Maya would be consumed in front of her. Reluctantly, she released her hold, and as she did so, the tendrils followed, white threads wrapping around her fingers, like tiny worms bouncing their heads off her skin. She stepped back. Small red dots speckled her arms. The tangle had been trying to take her as well.

She bent to the changeling. Its face was sloughing off, skin rotting, turning into black vegetal liquid. A bone, of wood, poked through flesh. Jessie gathered it carefully in her arms and walked up to the tangle presenting the changeling like an offering to an ancient, forgotten god. She knelt before mumbling prayers, promising the world, pledging anything if it would take the changeling and give Maya back.

The tendrils swayed as if caught by an invisible current, back and forth, wavering. But they did not stretch out for the changeling.

Jessie crawled forward, pressing the decaying, dripping mess forward, and this time the tendrils jerked away.

"You have to take it back. You have to. I never agreed to any of this. I want my daughter."

She shoved the rotten corpse forward and the tendrils whipped out, striking Jessie's arms so hard that lines of blood were drawn and she screamed, dropping what was left of the changeling to the ground with a broken squelch.

She wheeled around to Troy. "It won't take it. What are we supposed to do? How do we get Maya out?"

He ran his fingers through his hair, looking left and right.

"You're useless. You were supposed to help me figure this out. You were supposed to help me rescue Maya."

"I did what I could. What else am I supposed to do? I got you this far."

"You said it only takes unloved children. I love Maya. I love her with all my heart. I'd do anything to save her."

The tendrils stretched long to her again, tiny white heads dabbing at the bloody tracks on her arms. She could feel their intention. They wanted to drink her blood, wrap her up, consume her.

She did not move her arm. *What is the use?* she thought. If Maya was to die, why not die with her? The tendrils wrapped around her arms, small tubular bodies pulsing pink where they drew her blood.

"You need to get back," said Troy. "This thing's coming after you."

As they tasted her, she noticed a change in Maya. Her eyes opened, blinking, focus sharpening. The roots began to draw out of her, the tendrils slowly unwrapping. The tangle was letting her go.

Jessie caught Maya's gaze. Jessie's jaw trembled. This was what love was. This moment, this connection. All of her life, this is what had been missing and now she had found it.

"Troy, pick up Maya."

"But she's caught in there."

"Take her. Now. This is our chance to get her back. To free her."

Troy hesitated, glancing at the tendrils wrapping around Jessie's arms, the longer roots snaking across the floor towards her thighs.

"Troy, do it."

He stepped forward quickly, grimacing as filaments bounced across his face, as tiny razor mouths spun at his skin. He reached in, elbows deep into cancerous flesh and vegetative rot, and, for a moment, he tilted forward as if the tangle was about to inhale him, and then, suddenly he hopped backward, Maya in his arms.

"I've got her! Let's go. Run. Let's get out of here."

Jessie took another step towards the tangle. Grasses as sharp as razors sprouted from the fleshy ground cutting at her clothes, stripping her naked. Cold, wet creepers slithered up her legs, circling her waist.

"Jessie!"

She turned one last time to Troy, to her daughter, and smiled. Then she stepped into the tangle.

19

JESSIE-NOT-JESSIE TOUCHED the world with her roots. Deep beneath the earth, her roots spread far and wide, a vast network of capillaries and veins drawing in water and sustenance. Her roots grew, swimming through rich soil, muddy clay, winding alongside creeks, tendrils touching ancient oaks and redwoods through which she sensed the distant sun, the shifting clouds, the fog so heavy that it bent branches.

She swam through the world on those roots. She saw tadpoles emerging from glassy eggs in the submerged marsh grasses. She tasted the wind as it made the grasses whisper and whistle. She heard the clicking of beetles devouring the flesh of a kestrel fallen to earth.

She watched seeds unfurls, roots below, and stem above, and through them she experienced growth, expansion, pressing towards the heavens, the faces of flowers opening to the warm sun, energy bubbling in its cells, the falling of each petal, the drying of the stem, seeds forming within, and then everything falling apart, returning to slime, to black matter, to water, to the earth, and then the seed, with its code within, waiting for everything to be right again, for all that came before to start again.

She felt the steps of the raccoon on the dead leaf litter. She heard it scratching deeper into the hole in the ground, its tiny hands carving the earth, moving the soil. Its heartbeat shook against the earth, matching her own. She heard the squeal and the squirm of pink babies. Their dancing feet vibrated their joy to her.

Jessie-not-Jessie grew in her place, in that tangle. She was the swamp. She was the Dziwozona, the witch of the earth, the demon in the marsh. Her roots spread deeper, traveling, seeking, consuming, giving back.

Flesh mingled with mud, leaves with hair, wood with bone, water with blood.

She was everything and nothing. She was who she once had been, and she was no one.

She was once Jessie, and now no longer was.

She was the tangle, the swamp, the beckoning heard just beneath the wind.

She lay beneath the earth, in the tangle, was the tangle, her roots spread far and wide.

Sometimes the pain would return. The icy cold, the burning from heart to the tiniest of filaments. Oily water would seep to the surface. Her voice would rise above the winds and travelers in the night would swear they saw a shape, a woman cloaked, a woman bright and naked against the dark marsh grasses.

When the pain returned, Jessie-not-Jessie would stretch into her tendrils, dispersing herself and her consciousness, becoming the membrane.

She would listen to the earth and its passengers, those seeds that unfurled from the ground and melted back in black sludge. She would follow the network of her roots and tendrils and filaments until she found Maya again.

Maya, yes, Maya.

She stretched her roots across the membrane, through the goat trodden soil, and beneath the house, tendrils climbing between the walls, pale white shoots, blindly seeking, and she would find her daughter, laughing, loving, growing, a child who sometimes sat quietly on the front steps and looked to the west, to where the sun sank behind the ridge, to where the marsh waters pooled darkly.

And she would remember what she could not remember. She would hear the voice singing on the currents of the wind. She would feel the soft suck of the cold mud beneath her bare feet. She would remember herself not herself looking into her eyes, a mirror of what could have been. She remembered the tangle and the hands reaching for her, hands that held her with the greatest care.

Then those memories would thin like daylight cutting through the fog, burning it away, and all she was left with was an ache in her heart, as if something had been rooted there and now no longer was.

Jessie-not-Jessie touched the world with her roots.

FREE BOOK OFFER

Want to read the first book in the Hounds of the North fantasy series for free?

Join my email list at **www.peterfugazzotto.com** and get started on this action-packed dark fantasy series with *The Witch of the Sands*.

ACKNOWLEDGMENTS

Much of the inspiration for this story came from place, the ranches of West Marin, the waters of Tomales Bay, and the wild lands of Point Reyes National Seashore.

Thank you to early readers Evangeline Fugazzotto and Christine Harvey who helped reaffirm that I was on the right direction with the story.

Thanks to my dad for lending his copywriting expertise and reader's eye.

Finally, I want to thank Sara Chorn for a phenomenal job of editing my manuscript.

ABOUT THE AUTHOR

PETER FUGAZZOTTO is a writer of fantasy, horror, and science fiction. His short stories have been published in *Heroic Fantasy Quarterly*, *Grim Dark Magazine*, and *Far Fetched Fables*.

In addition to his writing, he earned a Black Belt in Brazilian Jiu Jitsu, once spent a summer vaccinating against yellow fever in the Amazon, and on his honeymoon stumbled upon a corpse flower in the jungles of Indonesia.

He lives in Northern California with his wife and daughter and an assortment of animals.

www.peterfugazzotto.com

Made in the USA
Monee, IL
27 July 2020